"Maybe We Ought To Have A Kid,"

Tyler suggested thoughtfully.

Kayla was startled. "We're divorced. Children should have two parents."

"I'd be around enough."

Kayla scoffed. "Mostly gone."

"Now, Kayla, you wouldn't want me to quit working and hang around the house…."

Again she mentioned, "We are divorced."

"You're an old-fashioned girl."

"I'm a current woman, and I am single. There is no way, at all, that I'd take on having a kid in this position. I'm not that careless."

He sighed into the phone. "So. I suppose we ought to be married."

"No thank you. We've tried that." And she hung up.

Dear Reader,

The celebration of Silhouette Desire's 15th anniversary continues this month! First, there's a wonderful treat in store for you as Ann Major continues her fantastic CHILDREN OF DESTINY series with November's MAN OF THE MONTH, *Nobody's Child.* Not only is this the latest volume in this popular miniseries, but Ann will have a Silhouette Single Title, also part of CHILDREN OF DESTINY, in February 1998, called *Secret Child.* Don't miss either one of these unforgettable love stories.

BJ James's popular BLACK WATCH series also continues with *Journey's End,* the latest installment in the stories of the men—and the women—of the secret agency.

This wonderful lineup is completed with delicious love stories by Lass Small, Susan Crosby, Eileen Wilks and Shawna Delacorte. And *next* month, look for six more Silhouette Desire books, including a MAN OF THE MONTH by Dixie Browning!

Desire…it's the name you can trust for dramatic, sensuous, engrossing stories written by your bestselling favorites and terrific newcomers. We guarantee handsome heroes, likable heroines…and happily-ever-after endings. So read, and enjoy!

Melissa Senate

Senior Editor

Please address questions and book requests to:
Silhouette Reader Service
U.S.: 3010 Walden Ave., P.O. Box 1325, Buffalo, NY 14269
Canadian: P.O. Box 609, Fort Erie, Ont. L2A 5X3

LASS SMALL
HOW TO WIN (BACK) A WIFE

SILHOUETTE *Desire*®
Published by Silhouette Books
America's Publisher of Contemporary Romance

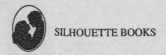 SILHOUETTE BOOKS

ISBN 0-373-76107-4

HOW TO WIN (BACK) A WIFE

LASS SMALL

finds living on this planet at this time a fascinating experience. People are amazing. She thinks that to be a teller of tales of people, places and things is absolutely marvelous.

One

It is now over five hundred years since TEXAS was first occupied by Europeans. The city of San Antonio has been altered and fooled with and adjusted. The downtown river is so lovely that it's been embellished and funneled into more loops.

The riverboat rides are especially nice. You get to see all the old trees, the clean water and the preserved buildings along the way.

One of those riverside buildings, by a handy iron curlicued bridge, harbors the law firm of Reardon, Miller and Rodriguez. The building was renovated inside, but the outside was preserved. The exterior was all painted subtly in a blue-tinted gray and the results are elegant.

Handily, the firm's office isn't far from the red granite Bexar County Courthouse. The red granite is the same granite that was used in Austin for the State Capitol. San Antonio has always been a little pushy.

The Bexar of Bexar County is pronounced "bear." Of course, in a long-ago motion picture that can still be seen on cable TV, Errol Flynn called the county "Bex-ar." Hearing that, the San Antonio people's eyes flinched and still do.

One of the Reardon, Miller and Rodriguez firm was Tyler Fuller. As a twenty-eight-year-old lawyer, he was a new rooster. He couldn't yet crow. He was again single.

The Fullers had been divorced for seven months, three weeks and two days. Tyler Fuller was not keeping track, he just happened to recall the time. After all, it had been *he* who had instigated the divorce.

It had stilled him with shock when the dark-haired, blue-eyed Kayla had discarded his name and gone back to her maiden name of Davie. She did that as if she'd wiped out everything about Tyler Fuller.

Kayla acted like there'd never been any good times—she hadn't seemed at all grieved to part from him. She'd flipped away like he'd never meant anything to her, at all.

When she got snippy and cold, and then moved out, he'd countered with the divorce. She hadn't turned a hair.

His parents, his siblings, his friends, even his kindergarten buddies all knew he was nuts.

Disgruntled, Tyler thought at least Kayla could have protested the divorce. She could have at least leaked a tear or two and looked at him with regret.

Tyler clearly remembered being in a group, not long after their divorce. He remembered having found her in the crowd and with casual élan he'd joined the segment which contained his ex-wife. With some assumed control, he'd used the excuse to be by her side by introducing Tom Keeper to her. Tom's family owned a chunk of West TEXAS.

Tyler had named Kayla as Kayla Fuller, and she'd given Tyler a glance as she'd corrected, "My last name's Davie."

Of course, her saying that had made Tom Keeper smile. Tom had been a male TEXAS predator of females since he was six months old. Everybody knew that. And after the introduction, Kayla had treated Tom as if he was harmless.

That just proved to Tyler that she needed some sort of chaperone. At twenty-five, she was a babe in the woods.

No normal woman would treat Tom like he wasn't dangerous. Any half-brained woman would have immediately known the real Tom Keeper's knuckles dragged on the floor and his pointed teeth dripped hot saliva.

It was just a good thing Tyler never left her side that night. He'd even told Tom that Kayla was still his as soon as she recognized that simple fact. Tom was not to foul up the works. Did he understand?

Tom had laughed. But he *had* gone on off...that night.

Tyler had known Kayla now for over four years. They were married not quite two years. And of the two years, they'd been divorced for seven months, three weeks and two days...exactly.

Just because they were divorced, she hadn't said

anything about their second anniversary. No card. No call. Nothing.

At the time, he'd courteously called so that she could thank him for the flowers. She hadn't answered her phone until after eleven. Where had she been on their anniversary? Grieving for their lost marriage, drinking rot gut in some sleazy bar?

Kayla was not a drinker. At best, she'd have two small glasses of wine in maybe three months. She wasn't any kind of drinker.

Where had she been on the night of their second anniversary?

He hadn't asked. He'd hinted several times, but he hadn't out and out asked. Actually, he'd pushed. She hadn't noticed.

They hadn't talked long on the phone. She'd been in a hurry. And she'd never once mentioned the milestone day. Of course, they were divorced. Even so, it seemed to Tyler that she should have remembered it had been two years since their wedding.

She hadn't been very open with him. When he'd finally talked to her that night, she'd asked, "Now what's the matter?"

And he'd said, "I just called to say—hello."

"It's after eleven, and I have to get to work early. Goodbye."

And she'd hung up! She had! On their second anniversary! It was probably a good thing they were already divorced.

Women are insensitive. It was always the man who bought the woman flowers, smoothed things between them and took the woman out to eat. And just because the eatery wasn't an Indiana Casa D'angelo! or a Café

Johnell, she'd slide her eyes around the place and her
face would be pinched.

Kayla wasn't at all sophisticated. She had no notion
as to how she ought to act. Once she'd gotten up from
the table and just flat out left a place. It was after a
guy had slid off the bar stool and lay on the floor...
ignored by the staff. But the staff was behind the bar,
and he had been short. The bartender probably
thought the guy had left.

Kayla had never considered the atmosphere—other
than to bury her nose in a lace-edged handkerchief.
Tyler *had* tried to expand her experiences, but she
was too limited. She did not accept variations.

How could a sixth-generation TEXAS woman be
so unknowing? She wasn't a delicate Easterner, she
was a solid TEXAS woman!

Tyler picked up the phone and punched the redial.
It rang in his ear twenty-four times. He hung up eventually. She probably was asleep and had turned off
the bell. No curiosity. She just lived her life in a vacuum.

Kayla really never did bend enough. She never had.
Like the dogfights. That night they'd found a gathering and stopped to see what it was. It was a dogfight
and he was curious. He'd said to her, "Just a minute."

It wasn't long before Tyler frowned and turned to
say they'd leave.

She was gone.

In that brief time, she'd vanished. She'd bought
four of the dogs at a staggering price and left the
place, taking them with her. There had been no room
for him in his car with her and the four dogs, and
without consulting him, she'd just...driven away!

Tyler was ticked. She'd abandoned him in that obnoxious place!

He'd had a couple of offers for rides, but the women had looked dangerous, so he'd walked.

At a public phone, he'd dialed the sheriff's office to alert him to the dogfights. By the time he got home, he was calm.

Kayla was asleep. Deep in their throats, the four dogs had growled a warning at him. None barked. They might waken her. Tyler had slept on the living-room sofa.

When he'd wakened the next morning, Kayla was gone. Gone. None of her clothes were in their closet. She'd moved out. She had taken the dogs.

She blamed him for the dogfights? That irritated him. She could have waited and listened. He was ticked.

Tyler had walked around. The apartment was silent. Even with all the furniture, the place was empty.

So he'd called at her parents' house. Obviously Kayla had contacted them with her side of the breakup. Her mother had said to Tyler, "Hello, dear. You've thrown it all at the fan."

Her mother was that way. She said outrageous things but she altered the words for politeness. Her mother was why Kayla was the way she was.

Kayla's dad was an observer. Although Mrs. Davie was open and clear, Mr. Davie was quiet, probably suspicious, and watched. That time he'd said to Tyler, "You goofed."

And Tyler had replied, "Not entirely."

As time passed, Tyler tried to get in touch with his wife, but she was never there. Her car was gone. No matter when he'd go past the Davie house, her car wasn't there. And she never answered the phone. The cook, Goldilocks, or her parents said, "I'm not sure where she is right now. I'll tell her you called."

So he had the divorce papers served. He'd thought that would stir her up.

She signed them.

Before Tyler knew what was really happening, he was divorced. Uncontested.

He got all the furniture except for the several pieces of antiques that had been in the Davie family for all eternity. She'd picked out their furniture. It was okay. Discreet. He'd have had the upholstery more colorful.

When he wasn't there, she'd come to their apartment and collected the rest of her things. But she'd left all of her keys.

There is nothing more irritating and deflating than a woman who won't fight to keep a man.

With all that furniture as his, his mother refused to have him back home, even briefly, so that he could heal. He had to stay where he was. But he didn't heal.

There wasn't a day dragged by that he wasn't aware Kayla wasn't there. She'd be back. She had a hungry body. She was ethereal. Pure. She wouldn't sleep around. He was her only partner in sex. She loved his body. She'd be back, and he'd explain.

He'd kept the place clean for seven months, three weeks and two days, waiting for her to open the door with her key and fling herself into his waiting arms.

No key. She'd left them all on the dining-room table. She didn't plan to...ever...come back.

She wouldn't even call him.

She never answered her phone. Just her mother. Or her father. Or one of her sisters. Or Goldilocks who ruled the Davie household but was supposed to just be the cook.

All of them just said Kayla wasn't there.

So…where was she?

They never knew.

She'd been abducted by aliens. No. There wasn't anything he could do about rescuing her from aliens in star ships. How about slave snatchers?

He'd go out in his cousin Wally's boat and chase down the bigger boat and rescue all the captives. But like Sean Connery in the film, Tyler would put Kayla into a rowboat and they'd drift away. He'd show her how they'd made love. She liked sex.

Kayla loved him.

When would she remember that?

When would her hungry body go on overdrive and force her to come back to him? She'd kick open the door, come inside and stand, looking at him with greed in her eyes. Her uncontrolled breasts would be heaving with her desire as her hot eyes would rake over him mercilessly. Yeah.

Then he found out she wasn't living at her parents' house, she was with a friend. She and those dogs. Henrietta was certainly a tolerant woman. She had cats.

Cats—and dogs who had been rescued from a *fighting pit?* That must be distracting. Who acted as umpire during the day when the humans were gone?

Kayla would come back to him.

He could handle dogs. He could handle women. He could handle her. Man! How he'd like handling her again. And he about went berserk at the very idea of it.

He always looked for her no matter where he was going. San Antonio wasn't *that* big. There were just over a million people. Eventually, he would get to run into her and then he'd exclaim, "I'm so sorry! Oh. Haven't we met?" And he'd laugh in his throat in the way that turned her on.

But he never once saw her. And he figured that she was grieving. She missed him so badly that she couldn't go out anywhere at all. She was zonked.

No other woman drew his eyes. He'd thought to date some classy babe and make Kayla jealous. But he couldn't. He looked at the laughing women and at their bodies, but none of them was Kayla. So he couldn't. He just couldn't. He could see no other woman. And he sighed.

His friends dragged him to different places where things would be mixed up and interesting. He was bored. He wandered around with an empty glass, and even knowing he wouldn't find her, he looked for Kayla.

There were men who mentioned, "Saw Kayla at the boxing match. She was on the first row and she was really involved."

Unbelievingly, Tyler's voice squeaked up as he exclaimed, "At a *boxing* match? She was *there?*"

The guy laughed. "Yeah. She's physical."

That froze Tyler's heart. How...physical had she been...with who all?

So the TEXAS winter came along. That's a whole lot like the Yankee spring. But in their winter, the thin blooded TEXANS put on jackets and complained about the cold.

It had snowed twice in Tyler's twenty-eight years. One of those times the snow had lasted two whole days before the TEXAS winter warmed enough to melt the miracle.

The native TEXANS said, "I don't understand those Yankees who winter down here. Those Winter TEXANS. They complain so about the northern snow! It's such a surprise and so pretty! How come the Yankees come down here instead of staying up yonder and enjoying the miracle?"

Now, how was a Winter TEXAN supposed to reply to that?

And for Tyler, time did pass. He worked hard at his office. When he was out, he found he could catch a glimpse of Kayla now and again. Or someone who might have been she. Someone who walked like Kayla…who wasn't. Several times in those months, he'd run after a woman and then awkwardly apologized.

One of those mistakes had grinned and waited for him to make some move to know her. But Tyler's disappointment had been such that he couldn't see the woman as a woman. She just wasn't Kayla.

Tyler Fuller was a lawyer. The firm Reardon, Miller and Rodriguez had about fifty lawyers downtown. There were branches of the firm in other locations.

Tyler was in an awesome firm in which he was just a growing mushroom. He was under a woman lawyer who was only eight years older than he. She was Barbara Nelson. And she was not married. Not that marriage would have slowed her down any.

Barbara's secretary handed out work and some was given to Tyler. A buck slip or a route slip was on the document for information.

Through her secretary, Barbara Nelson had Tyler

drafting documents, writing briefs, handling the background for labor disputes, Social Security disability petitions and interviews with clients or opponents.

All the problems were run-of-the-mill except for the persons involved. The problems could be divorce, bankruptcy, or pretrial motions or interviews with prospective witnesses.

Some days, Tyler might have to go to the police station and check files, or see doctors who had pro or con evidence. Tyler was busy.

His secretary was from the firm's pool. And he tried always to get Marian Web because she was so brilliant that she never made a mistake nor did she allow him to make any. She was his mother's age and tolerant of Tyler. That was clear when she adjusted her commitments so that she could mostly help Tyler.

Women spoiled him rotten.

Well, some women.

His immediate boss, Barbara Nelson, was thirty-six years old. She was a single woman who had control, and she was in charge. She was confident, selective, and she was blunt. She didn't chew tobacca. That was a plus.

Tyler had no real qualms about her until his divorce. Then, once, the Nelson woman had patted his bottom! He'd been offended.

She'd always smiled at Tyler and watched his body when he was walking toward her. His sex loved it. His brain was offended. But she hadn't approached him until just after his divorce.

She'd say, "Let's have a drink after work."

He'd ask, "Is this important? There's batting practice." Tyler *was* on the legals' baseball team. And she wouldn't find out if what he said was true. That's why he'd never used the excuse of a business appointment. She could check it out.

With his baseball-used rejection, Barbara had smiled and told him, "Since we work together, I just thought it would be nice…to get acquainted."

He lied to her with great grief-stricken eyes, "I'm going to a shrink. I can't handle this divorce."

So Barbara had half lowered her eyelids as she said, "Let me know when you're more…open."

His sex bulged, his back shivered and his throat clacked as he said, "Yes." And he got away.

Again Tyler had lied. He had no notion of ever getting involved with that woman. She terrified him. And he began to understand the slender woman in the secretary pool who wore high neck, bulky clothes and no makeup and kept her face blank and serious with her eyes downcast.

It was only then Tyler realized—what was her name? It was Martha. Martha never said one word. She had to've talked some time. But she had no casual or friendly chatter to share.

He went to Martha and told her, "Help me. Pretend you and I are a couple. No! I promise I'll leave you alone. I'm just divorced. I don't want any ties. Pretend we're good friends."

"Leave me alone."

That's what she said.

And she didn't wait until he replied. Martha was brief and finished. She'd said it all.

Tyler was out on a raft in a dangerous sea and no one but the sharks were aware of him.

Even men have it rough. That was a revealing and startling observation. Up until then, Tyler had thought men had it all. That men controlled the world and their own lives as they chose. How the world... changes.

Tyler didn't have a whole lot of trouble in seeming to be solemn. He simply didn't laugh. He didn't join the groups that stood and chatted. He kept to himself, harboring, nurturing his grief.

So John Reardon, who was the Big Gun of the Firm, called Tyler into his office. That was a shock. Tyler's mind went over everything he'd done and wondered where he'd fouled up.

He was on time at Mr. Reardon's appointment. He sat in the outer office, and the secretary smiled at him. She said, "We don't see much of you anymore."

He looked at her...her name was Nancy. He said, "Yeah."

"Mr. Reardon will be free in a minute. He just wants to know if you're okay. You used to be so funny. Since your divorce, you've gotten so quiet that we all worry about you."

She was kind to tell him why he was there. A whole lot of knots loosened in his body and he could relax a little. But he didn't smile. Fortunately, he'd been so panicked that he didn't yet smile. So he could control it.

Nancy said, "All of us are worried about you. I thought we ought to have a party for you. A freedom party, now that you're single again. But Mr. Reardon said, 'Not yet.' So we'll wait until you can enjoy it...too." She grinned at him.

His smile was a little sick. In an office as big as theirs was, how could any one of them have the time to notice somebody like him? It was touching in a way, but it made Tyler feel as if he was on a stage, alone...without a script.

He'd never realized anyone in the firm had noticed him. Other than his boss, Barbara Nelson.

He'd lived in a secure niche of anonymity while he was married. Now, divorced, he was loose and vulnerable. He began to understand women who were in the same slot he was in then. He understood Martha's bundled-up clothing and her lack of animation.

His meeting with Mr. Reardon was longer than necessary. Tyler had work to do. He was a little restless.

"I know how you feel," Mr. Reardon told Tyler. "I've been where you are now. It's been some years ago, but that doesn't soften such a happening. I know just exactly what you're going through."

So Mr. Reardon got to go through it all again. It was too much. As empathetic as the top gun was, Tyler was busy. He had work to do. No two situations are ever the same. No one knows what another suffers. Mr. Reardon had had an affair, and his first wife had found out.

Tyler had had no affair. All that he'd done was to try to expand Kayla's knowledge of adventures. She'd misunderstood, been ungrateful and stubborn. Women are a great nuisance.

There is no substitute for women.

That was a very sobering realization. A man married, and that was it! He had a partner for life. To have and to hold. And she'd wiggled away from him and was gone!

Then Tyler heard that Mr. Reardon was saying with

a sigh, "It happens. You'll get through this in time. We're all backing you. Chin up!"

And Tyler was touched. Whatever the big man had been saying, he meant to help. Tyler rose and stood tall. "Thank you, sir."

Mr. Reardon inquired kindly, "You sure you don't want a couple of days off?"

"No, sir." Tyler was startled. Had the old man been trying to give him some time off? He said earnestly, "I'd like to get things done." Then he added gently, "Mother says a man needs distraction. Law is surely that."

"Yes, my boy. You're a good man." Reardon nodded in agreement with his words. "I'm glad we have you with us. If there's ever any problem, just let us help."

"Thank you, sir." And Tyler was surprised to find his eyes were moist.

It got worse when Mr. Reardon stood up and came around the desk to put an arm over Tyler's shoulders. "I'm glad we had this talk. Remember, you're one of us."

Really touched, Tyler almost choked on his emotions. "Thank you, sir."

"I'm here, my boy. Anytime."

And he escorted Tyler to the door where they shook hands.

Imagine that. Tyler walked unseeing down the corridor. Just imagine that whole place being aware of one little, wet-eared lawyer. He was brilliant, of course, but not everyone of the firm had that knowledge, as yet.

He went back to his desk and sat down in the shared office.

His office mate was Jamie Oliver. Jamie asked, "Everything go okay?"

And Tyler swung his chair around and said with the amazement he felt, "The old man wanted to know if I'm okay."

"You foul up something? How can I help?"

And Tyler laughed. But he was again touched. Even Jamie was on his side. Not even competitive! He just asked to help. And Tyler's eyes got wet again.

Jamie got up and came over very seriously to lean down. "What is it?"

"They wanted to help me get through this problem with Kayla. It's been a while. They thought I needed help. I turned down a drink with Nelson."

Jamie frowned at Tyler. "That was rash. I'd jump at any chance like that."

Tyler laughed. "'You're a better man than I, Gunga Din.'"

"I know." And Jamie walked back to his chair, sat, rolled his chair in to his desk and was immediately absorbed in the papers.

That evening with his parents, Tyler told his dad about the firm's head honcho. "I was surprised. It never occurred to me anyone else would understand."

"We all understand," his dad assured his son. "Have you seen the darlin' lately?"

Well, Tyler surely knew Kayla was the "darlin'" mentioned. And he was a little irritated to have her called a darling. She was the one who'd left him. A bit stilted, Tyler replied, "No."

His father sighed rather too heavily and lamented, "How did you let her get away?"

And, unfortunately, Tyler snapped, "I was only trying to educate her and—" But he didn't get to explain.

His father looked up at his own son in aghast shock! "You *hurt* her?"

"No! Good gravy, Dad! I took her to see what had garnered such a crowd and found out there was a dogfight! I'd never seen one and thought she would be curious, too."

And his father's face changed from alarm to indignation. "You took that fragile flower to a *dogfight?*" His voice squeaked up rather remarkably. "They're illegal."

And with seriousness, Tyler went on. "I know that. I've contacted the state police. I've offered to be a witness." He was deadly. "She was not frightened. She bought four of the dogs and put them in the car. I had to walk home!"

His father stared for the count of three, then his closed mouth stretched out, his body began to jiggle and after that the laughter rolled.

Tyler stood trying to get in some logical, adult information. But with the hilarity of his father's misguided sense of humor, Tyler finally gave up. He left his parents' house, slammed the door, shaking the entire, bulky structure, and went to his own apartment.

Then he went back for his car and drove it to the apartment. He turned off the phone bell and in spite of his lengthy walk to retrieve his car, he had one hell of a time trying to calm down and sleep that night.

Now, how and why was it that everyone in the sprawled-out city of the diversified San Antonio learned what that Fuller family conversation had been? Guess.

Even the whisperings and giggles and guffaws at the office were to be endured. In just a couple of days, look at the turnaround of the whole layout of his life...from compassion to hilarity.

Tyler was sober, businesslike and he ignored the snorts of laughter. The only one who showed any sympathy, at all, was his office mate, Jamie.

Jamie said, "Sometime, when you can handle it, I'll tell you what happened to me. But from my own experience, I can give you this—you'll live. Ignore the pack. They have little sunlight in their lives. You've given them this magic moment." Jamie never looked up from his computer. His voice was moderate. He did not laugh.

Oddly, the joke on Tyler eased all the firm people's acquired facade. What had happened to Tyler was worse than most of what had happened to them. Such a public put-down as he'd had made Tyler vulnerable. And they all understood vulnerability.

But it made his boss, Barbara Nelson, eager to soothe Tyler.

Out of the frying pan and into the fire.

He complained to Jamie.

Jamie said, "She can soothe me."

Distracted, irritated, Tyler said, "I'll tell her."

"Get my name right. She calls me Johnny."

So Tyler explained her mistake. "People in control of many others have some difficulty with names."

"She sure as hell knows yours."

"I'm divorced, so I'm not a wet-nosed kid. She expects me to know the ropes?"

Jamie smiled. He licked his lips and put his lower lip under his teeth but he didn't reply or embellish anything.

He made Tyler laugh.

What a time it was. His longing for Kayla. His adjustment at the office. The adjustment of the co-workers to him. Their now knowing who he was because of all the problems he was having. And it was all because of one woman. Kayla. Kayla Davie who chose to discard Tyler's name.

That Kayla Davie Fuller was due a set down. Any woman her age ought to be more pliant than she was. She acted as if she had all her life to find a good man. One better than Tyler.

What man was better than he?

Two

Especially in big cities, there are little sections or groups of people who are isolated by their jobs or interests or kinship. Each segment believes they are The City. They're the important ones. It's mental territory.

It is solely for them that the city puts on the park festivals, the food tastings, the bands playing and the marching parades. It is all done only for their segment's own entertainment.

The other people who are there are just phantom people.

The actual citizens who live among friends hardly ever even see the phantoms who are busily involved in their own lives and their own groups. Well, they don't see them unless some hungry eyes are looking for someone of the opposite sex. Then they see *everybody!*

But mostly a group sees only those in their own group, and they ignore the many others who are all unseen shadows. The phantom ones drive cars and walk streets and go to grocery stores and to their cleaners.

The phantoms are like elevator background music. They are there to fill in the edges of lives so that no one believes he's alone. The phantoms are busy with things to be done.

So are those busy people who think they are so special that the world is really just theirs. To those who believe they are the ones in control, the world is for them. Simple. That is true. But *all* the segments of people think that way. It is their own group that is the important, vibrant, needed one.

For those isolated, self-contained groups, the strangers' houses might just as well be empty. The unknowns' offices are blank. The other people in the restaurants don't count. Not unless you're looking and then those strange ones are real but unknown others.

Few people think about all those unknown others who live in the city and move about. They don't really matter unless they get into some kind of trouble. Then everybody helps. Helping isn't thought out, it is reaction.

Such thinking was just so, for those who were involved with Tyler and Kayla.

Their friends and kinfolk talked to each other about the divorced pair. At a remote family wake, one cousin of Tyler's mother said of the divorced pair, "I do declare I've never seen any couple so hostile to each other. Even Cousin Douthet didn't carry on *this* badly. I've no patience with the two of them."

"Hush! Tyler is right over there, and he can hear you!"

The cousin pinched her mouth as she lifted her eyebrows and looked down without moving her head. "Listening to me just might do him some good."

And at her side, a male voice inquired softly, "What would you say to him?"

It was Tyler himself who spoke. So his mother's Cousin Maren replied, "You ought to've been talking to that child, all along. She's a Davie, and you let her get away from you!"

"I wasn't there when she left." Well, he was asleep...on the sofa in the living room. But he had the audacity to add, "I had no choice."

And Cousin Maren replied, "Once *I* left Hebert!" She raised staying hands and turned her head aside. Although no one said anything, Cousin Maren held up her hands as if they'd all gasped and protested such an act. She went on: "And Hebert came to Daddy's house and said, 'You get her out here as quick as you can!'"

Tyler inquired, "And, did your daddy do that?"

"No."

So Tyler asked, "What'd Cousin Hebert do?"

"He came into my room and said to me, 'Get your things together, woman, I've used up my patience with you.'"

"He said *that?*" It was Tyler, himself, who exclaimed. Of course, Tyler had heard her husband's version so he was interested in this one.

And Cousin Maren replied, "I stood firm and lifted my chin." She showed them how she'd done that. "And I pointed to my doorway and told Hebert, 'Leave here.' But he would not.

"I finally had to go down and open the front door for him. He then picked me up and carried me to his car. My daddy tried to help me, but Hebert wouldn't allow that."

Tyler was the only new listener. All the others had heard Cousin Maren's version, in its varieties, for some time, by then.

And with some unkind humor, Tyler asked, "Did you ever escape again?"

Cousin Maren sighed and looked off sadly. "I never managed. Hebert is such a determined man."

So Tyler offered, "I'll come help you the next time."

There were coughs that covered the listeners' shocked hilarity.

But then Maren looked up at Tyler, and he saw that she was not loved as she wanted. Hebert had never cherished her as she'd needed. So she had made up what she wanted.

With earnest compassion, Tyler told his mother's cousin, "He was lucky your daddy couldn't stop him, and he got you back. You're a jewel."

Her eyes filled with tears, and Tyler hugged her.

As she leaned into his arms, the old lady asked, "How could Kayla ever have left you?" And she looked up at Tyler's eyes with such remorse.

The odd thing about that little vignette was that it didn't just joggle Tyler's understanding, but it surprised the watchers who'd never before realized Cousin Maren was so vulnerable. It made them all think and, after that, they were kinder to her.

But the experience touched Tyler. He'd been deliberately pushing the edge with the old lady. He was acting that way to amuse the watchers. How strange to realize the old cousin wasn't a joke; she was human and she needed attention.

So Tyler searched the noisy crowd out to find Cousin Hebert and told him very seriously, "Your wife needs some civil attentions from you. You need to admire her and hold her hand and be kind."

Cousin Hebert squinted his eyes at Tyler and asked, "What all've you been drinking, boy? I want some of that."

Tyler became very serious and settled in to educate the eighty-one-year-old cousin, in women. Tyler was earnest and kind.

Cousin Hebert protested, "I'm too old for that stuff, boy! I can't even get up on a horse no more."

Earnestly, Tyler coaxed, "You can share the sunset with her. You can see to it that she's comfortable. You can buy her something little, and you can give her a rose—"

But after a while, Hebert just asked, "How long since your wife left you?"

Sadly, Tyler said, "Too long."

And Cousin Hebert said, "How come she left?"

"Damned if I know."

"I guess you wasn't doing something you ought to've been doing?"

"I don't know what that is."

And Cousin Hebert suggested, "Ask her."

With great sadness, Tyler told the old man, "I haven't been able to get in touch with her."

But Cousin Hebert said, "Maybe you ought to try harder?"

"I suppose."

It's strange how events turn around and can be viewed from another angle. While Tyler didn't budge

Cousin Hebert one quarter inch, Tyler was budged into finding out why Kayla hadn't come back to him. She had not only avoided him, she hadn't even spoken to him.

Why had she so carefully made herself unavailable to him? That was the part that hurt Tyler so terribly. She no longer wanted to see him. That made his feeling of self-worth fade.

He wasn't a...hero anymore. He was just a man.

About the only thing that kept Tyler Fuller going was the baseball team. It had been organized by the legal firms there in San Antonio. From among the various firms, they had rival teams. There were a whole lot of snide comments about lawyers playing baseball.

Even the lawyers said those kind of things to one another.

And one of the first problems was when the women lawyers and secretaries and receptionists had insisted on playing baseball with the men. It hadn't worked. The men used different bats and the baseballs were hard. So the female players gradually moved to playing separate games.

And last season the women in the Reardon firm won the area's legal cup. And the male segment of the firm scored second...to last.

However, being enlightened, the men set up an elegantly structured table in the lobby of their building and put the women's cup on the table with a spotlight. The table was exactly the right size to show off the cup. It wasn't too small or skimpy and it wasn't hu-

mongous to overwhelm the cup. It was a perfect ex-
hibit. That soothed a lot of ruffled feathers.

It had been Barbara Nelson's idea. It was she who
had suggested it to the men. She'd expected a hoopla
of objection, but the men fooled her. It had been a
good move. When Tyler had commented positively
on the cup, his boss, Barbara Nelson, had just smiled
at him.

Even though he'd been married, then, that smile
had scared Tyler more than anything else. Hers was
a predator's smile.

On the team, Tyler played second base. He did well
enough as a batter but he had never hit a home run.
He was alert and quick. He did his share and he was
accurate in his throws. Probably the best thing was
that he looked. He knew where players were and he
threw precisely. He was a plus. He kept his eye on
the ball.

Probably the best advice he got on playing ball was
from his great-uncle Clyde, who said, "Whenever a
baseball referee mentions your number, shake your
head in a serious, surprised way. Everybody will think
the referee was as blind as they'd always suspected."

That small move could also be applied to a lawyer's devaluation of another lawyer's client in court.
Especially if there was a jury.

Last year, Kayla had been one of the wives who'd
come out to the games. She'd been interested and
ornery. She'd laughed when the crowd got too upset
over anything. She'd been weird even then.

Tyler groaned as he contemplated how he missed
her. As the games were played, he'd foolishly look
in the stands for her. And he'd realize she was gone.

He had no one to cheer him on and give him the knowledge that somebody cared about him.

His parents were there. His sisters and brothers and nieces and nephews. His cousins... Yeah. And they cheered. But Kayla wasn't there.

Even Barbara Nelson was there. She would be. She made Tyler's skin prickle in alarm.

It was after a while and months of trying before Tyler finally got hold of his ex on the phone. He was so surprised when she answered that for a breath he couldn't think of anything to say.

She'd repeated, ''Hello?''

And he'd said, ''Don't hang up.''

Her impatient sigh had been obvious. But she hadn't hung up.

He'd said, ''I need to know that you're all right.''

''Yes.''

''And I need to know if you need anything at all. Do you have enough money?''

''Yes.''

He'd scrambled for something to say. ''Is your car working all right?''

''Yes.''

''I miss you like bloody hell.''

''You'll get over it.''

''Now, Kayla, that wasn't nice at all. You could've said you miss me a little.''

''I bought all those other dogs.''

''Other? You didn't *have* a— You mean me.''

''I've never seen anyone who went such places as you chose.''

''I was curious. It wasn't for long.''

"I doubt it. I must go. Have I replied to all your questions?"

"You aren't out watching the games. I miss you in the bleachers."

In surprise, she did gasp but then she'd said flippantly, "I'm busy."

"Who're you busy—with?"

"The Davies are having their annual picnic. I'm helping get it organized."

"It was fun last year. Since I'm—was married to you, do I get to go this year?"

"No."

He had coaxed, "We had a good time last year."

"How nice."

"Let's have coffee tomorrow. I'll come by your office and get you."

She wasn't encouraging. "I'll be busy."

"Not…that…busy. We need to talk."

"My other phone's ringing. Take care."

And she'd hung up.

Oddly enough, the stiff, aloof exchange had made Tyler exuberant! It was the first time she'd talked to him in a long while!

His counterself had said a sour: Goody.

And he'd replied to his counterself, *Well, we exchanged words. Those were the first exchanged words that weren't about divorce!*

In spite of his counterself, Tyler had gone to bed that night with a smile. His dreams had been erotic. He'd been faithful. He had dreams. He wakened with the stimulation. And he lay and wondered if that hungry body of hers dreamed like his. His sex was named

Godzilla. Yeah. He'd done the naming at age fourteen. Half his lifetime ago.

At the office, since his divorce, he referred to Barbara as Miss Nelson...relentlessly.

She told him, "You needn't be so formal."

He smiled at her and replied, "I'm being formal.
You're my boss. To call you by your name would
sound pushy."

"I don't mind...pushy."

"It isn't businesslike and respectful." He was ad-
amant. So he went right on calling Barbara, Miss Nelson.

For a while she sassed back by calling Tyler, Mr.
Fuller. But he accepted that term with a slight, serious
nod. So she went back to calling him Tyler.

If Barbara had been any younger she would have
torn her hair. But she just waited.

For Tyler, her waiting was a whole lot like realizing a big spider knew where he was and was watching
him from some crack in the wall. It was scary.

He shared that fear with Jamie.

Jamie said, "Tell me which crack, and I'll take care
of it for you." Jamie said that not even looking up
from his papers.

So Tyler told Barbara, "Jamie admires you."

And she asked, "Jamie...who?"

Tyler blinked. She really *didn't* know which man
was Jamie. So Tyler was gentle. "We share an office.
He's Jamie Oliver. A fine lawyer. He looks at you
with admiration."

Barbara slitted her eyes and watched Tyler but she
didn't respond, so he went off. He could feel Barbara

Nelson's eyes under his clothes all the way down the hall. He shivered.

So then Barbara-who-was-now-referred-to-as-Miss Nelson met Tyler in the hall. She asked Tyler to lunch with her.

But he said earnestly, "I've a meeting with Kayla. She has a problem."

He hadn't even said thank you or looked directly at the woman. And he just went on off down the hall.

And he didn't dare to look back to see if the prickles down his backside were actually from her lascivious stare.

He called Kayla at work and said, "If you have any sense of compassion at all, you'll have lunch with me today. That barracuda who is Barbara Nelson has her eye on me."

In a dead voice, his ex-wife said with no emphasis at all, "How exciting."

"Don't be nasty. You could help out a little. You owe me something."

"I owe *you* something? I do not!"

"Kayla, you are the most compassionate woman I've ever known. I'm not asking you to come back home and get into my bed—" And the very idea of her doing that ruined his breathing. He was silent.

She sighed into the mouthpiece and said, "Okay. This once."

He left his office early to avoid walking out with Miss Nelson...and having her glued to him for the lunch hour...with Kayla. No way.

At the bank, Tyler went to Kayla's office before she was ready to leave it, and he sat patiently in the waiting room until Kayla came to fetch him.

Kayla groused, "Everybody in the building knows

you're here! They all think we're bonding. This has got to be the last time I see you."

"Why?"

And Kayla sighed with great patience and reminded Tyler, "We're divorced!"

He told her logically, "We married because there is a bond between us. WE understand each other—"

"Oh, no, we don't!"

"—most of the time." He had continued. "You tend to be more structured in your conduct and not open to new ideas—"

"I will not see you again!"

"—but we are friends." He finished his words.

Kayla was positive, "No. We are not."

With legal logic, Tyler was firm. "We were friends in our marriage. And we were lovers. I want to continue the friendship."

She scoffed, "You want a shield. You can't handle one woman, much less two."

Their argument continued all the way down the street and into the restaurant, through the line as they chose what they wanted, to their table and all the way through their lunch. It was like old times. What else can a woman expect from a lawyer? He argues all the time!

Tyler cheerfully walked Kayla back to her building. He would have escorted her to her desk, but she was firm that he did not.

So that night at the park's baseball diamond, Tyler batted in two runs. He was thrown out both times. But the team cheered the runs. At least Tyler had helped somebody else make it to home plate.

But Kayla wasn't in the bleachers. He looked. He

watched. He almost missed a ball. He settled down, accepted that she wasn't there and he played baseball.

At the office, at that time, Tyler's primary concern was drafting the contracts for a hospital, which was buying out a doctor's private medical practice. This was done under Miss Nelson's watch. The hospital would put the doctor on their payroll as a full-time employee. The hospital would bill the patients, and the doctor would rotate with the other doctors in being available on night call and weekends.

While it was interesting to Tyler, he felt some hesitancy for the doctor. However, he was again impressed with Miss Nelson's ability and knowledge. She was a superior mentor.

She scared him spitless.

The contract would take about a week to finalize the draft to present to the hospital for their input. Somebody at the firm would meet with the hospital authorities to agree on the final version.

The hospital would then present the contract to the doctor, who would consult his own lawyer. His lawyer could make suggestions for changes. After that was done, she would return the contract to the hospital.

The hospital then might or might not agree to the changes. And they would have to have a meeting. If there were no changes they could sign the contract. If there were changes and the hospital agreed with them or the parties agreed with some modification, they would ask the law firm to include the modified changes into the contract. Then it would be ready for execution.

The entire process was interesting to Tyler. He

found it stimulating to smooth people's problems and help them. His mind worked differently from nonlegal minds. He always considered ramifications.

He had decided against being a candidate for any local or federal political office. He had given the idea thoughtful consideration. A political career wasn't for him. He was a home boy. But he could help a candidate. He'd help somebody he believed in.

And he found it was annoying that Kayla wasn't there as his sounding board. She had taken that position since he'd first known her.

She'd taken other positions since then. Now her position was to be gone from him. What an irritating woman! Why couldn't she be pliant and fascinated like she was supposed to be? Instead she was out of his life, on her own and not needing him around!

It was depressing to understand an ex-wife didn't need him any longer. She adjusted well to being on her own. Actually, she wasn't entirely. She and her dogs were sharing a place with Henrietta and her cats.

So one noon who should Tyler run into on the street but Henrietta! He smiled his smile of greeting women and didn't look at her chest. He said, "Well, how's it going?"

Henrietta grinned. "Great! Thanks for getting me a new roomie."

Sourly, Tyler replied, "I didn't have anything at all to do with Kayla leaving me. I'm trying to get her back."

"I don't think she'd be interested."

"We'll see. How are the dogs and cats getting along?" And his eyes were cool as he waited for her reply.

But Henrietta said airily, "We got rid of the dogs

before she even moved in. Most were prime dogs. They were snatched up. One of the prime ones went with his original owner! We couldn't find where they'd stolen the other dogs.''

''I thought Kayla bought those dogs.''

''Oh, she did. And she got her money back. But the dogs had been stolen. Well, one hadn't.''

Tyler frowned. ''I didn't know the dogs had been stolen.''

''Haven't you ever seen the papers when the pit dogs are killed by an opponent, the pit people then drive through the city and just leave the dead dogs in an alley somewhere?''

''Poor dogs.''

''They use female dogs, in heat, to lure the male dogs away from the owners' yards.''

''Females have always been a trial for males. Even dogs.''

Henrietta laughed, gave Tyler a casual wave and went on off down the street.

Tyler walked along to a café for lunch. He was deliberately alone. With a group a man can't offer to sit down with a single woman. He needed a woman. Actually, he needed Kayla. Even going alone this way, he wasn't really interested in finding another woman to be permanent. He wanted to talk and be listened to.

He went through the lunch line not seeing anyone he knew. The place was Nick's. The owner was named Bob. The place had been Nick's for something like thirty years. Tyler greeted Bob, didn't see Tim wave to him and went to a table with one woman.

No rings. Not bad looking. Slender. Reading a book. She needed company.

Tyler inquired with courtesy, "Vacant?" And he indicated the chair across from her.

She looked up from her book to look only at the chair. She said, "Nobody's around. You can have it." And she went back to her book.

She didn't say one word to Tyler. She didn't even look at him. He felt like a ghost. Women looked at Tyler. He was always careful to only smile and never wink. Winking can get a man in trouble.

His table partner went on reading. He tried to see what the book was. Not a clue. He asked, "What's the book about?"

She briefly looked up and said, "Huh?" But she instantly went back to the book.

That's a put-off. So Tyler didn't try for dialogue.

It was diminishing to have a book be more interesting than being a man like he was. He asked for the salt.

Blindly, she handed it to him from the middle of the small table. She didn't look up from the book.

He pretended to salt everything without salting anything. He didn't tilt the shaker but he moved his hand up and down as if he was salting it all. She never looked up. Then he put the shaker in the middle of the table. He asked, "Why is the book so interesting?"

"I'm on my lunch hour."

Tyler narrowed his eyes. That was another put-off. She was on her lunch hour therefore she didn't need to discuss anything with a stranger.

She ate and read. Tyler sat silently and ate. He looked around somewhat. No one was staring at him with knowledgeable sneers. People went on with their lives not needing to know what Tyler Fuller was doing or how he was doing or if he was deliberately being ignored by another indifferent woman.

It's diminishing to realize no one really cares about a recently divorced man.

He remembered the sci-fi motion picture of *The Shrinking Man.* Tyler's clothes still fit. He could sit on a chair. He wasn't actually shrinking.

That was something to be thankful about. He drew a breath that was rather sad. She didn't look up. A man could sigh that sadly and that heartless woman didn't even have the courtesy to ask what was the matter. What was the world coming to?

So Tyler took the long way back to the office. He told Jamie, "I met a woman at lunch."

Jamie never glanced up. He replied, "I saw her."

Tyler silently sat down at his desk. Jamie had seen the reading woman who'd never even once looked at Tyler.

Tyler picked up some papers and began to read them for errors. He went back and began again. He finally actually began to read.

Three

One assignment, for Tyler, was research for a company that was considering leasing space in a shopping center, there in San Antonio. For their client, Tyler was to examine the proposal for loopholes in the lease. He would study what it took to terminate the contract if that should be needed.

Tyler would find what remedies there were if the lessor didn't keep the stated promises. He would see whether the lessor cleaned and repaired the rented areas. And he would find how the rental fees compared with what the other tenants in the center paid, and how the rents there compared to those at other shopping centers.

Not only rents were compared, but also the fees the lessor charged for advertising the shopping center and what advertising media he used. And Tyler was to check if the parking lot was also attractive, neat, cared for and repaired.

Tyler would not be the one to negotiate the contract. That would be done by other lawyers in the firm who had more business experience. But Tyler would sit in on those negotiations and learn how it was done.

He was still in the "gofer" category. Just about everything he was assigned to do was a…learning experience.

And for all such research, Tyler reported to his superior, Barbara Nelson, whom he tenaciously called Miss Nelson. He asked a whole lot of questions of his office buddy, Jamie Oliver. Jamie had been there longer.

And there were times when Jamie replied, "You'll have to ask Barb."

"How can you call her Barb so carelessly?"

And Jamie who rarely looked up from his papers replied, "She doesn't see me."

Thoughtfully, Tyler suggested, "It's probably because she hasn't the nerve to attack you. She yearns for you and dreams of you."

"I wish."

And with some compassion for the ignored office mate, Tyler said, "She probably tries to lure me just to get your attention."

That made Jamie laugh. He even glanced up. His eyes were dancing with lights of amusement.

Tyler thought of Jamie and wondered why Miss Nelson didn't see the man. Maybe it was because Jamie never looked up but was so engrossed in law that Miss Nelson thought Jamie didn't see *her*.

Kindly, Tyler advised, "You ought to spend more time out at the water cooler."

"The staff gets too friendly."

Tyler blinked once. Then he replied, "You're too selective."

"Want a date with a friend of mine who admires you?" Jamie again glanced at Tyler!

Tyler sighed and shook his head as he went back to his own papers.

Jamie told Tyler, "See? You, too, are selective. Mattie would spread her knees for you by the water cooler, she's so smitten."

"Who is this...Mattie? I've never heard of her."

"That's how Barb is with me. She can't see me."

And kindly, Tyler told Jamie, "She's too old for you."

"Two years. I taught for four years before I went to law school."

And Tyler gasped, "You're over thirty?" His voice even squeaked up.

"Yep. I've crossed the Great Divide."

"Holy Moses."

And Jamie agreed. "It's awesome."

"Have you told Miss Nelson how old you are?"

"She probably likes her men young and fresh."

"I've been *married!*"

Jamie grinned, closemouthed, and bit his lower lip. That was to stop himself from commenting. And he immediately went back to work. But he was still irritatingly amused because he gently coughed a couple of times to hide his snorts of laughter.

So Barbara called Tyler to her office. And he had no choice. He went like a cat going into dog territory. He was alert, intense and very formal.

He didn't jump up onto the top of the bookcases.

He didn't even sit. He said, "Yes?" And he carried a folder and a pencil.

Tyler wore the fake eyeglasses he'd taken up just recently. He had perfect sight and the glasses were only regular glass. He thought they made him look more aloof, unapproachable and withdrawn.

He looked young.

Barbara smiled and said, "I'll need the folder on the Bennett's lease tomorrow. Are you finished with it?"

Tyler's heart was in his mouth. She would ask him to stay after hours. She had a leather couch in her office. He was vulnerable. What would he say?

Barbara went on, "Molly can't stay tonight, so you won't have a typist available. As I recall, you have a computer at home? You can take the brief home and get it done there. I'll come by between nine and ten and collect it then. Okay?"

She was going to come to his apartment! There was no out. Tyler very seriously nodded—once.

Barbara smiled and said, "See you then." And she returned to the papers on her desk.

Tyler woodenly walked from her office and went back down the hall to the one he shared with Jamie.

Having sat at his desk, Tyler turned to Jamie and said, "Jamie. Miss Nelson is coming to my place tonight to fetch a brief I will finish on my computer at home. Can you—"

And Jamie said, "It's your problem. I have other plans for tonight."

"It would be your big chance! You could go out and pull her spark plugs and her car wouldn't work and you could take her home!"

"Sorry. And I really am. But I have another interview tonight."

Cautiously, Tyler inquired, "Interview?"

And Jamie replied readily, "A smaller firm. I've learned all I can from this one."

"Don't leave me here alone!"

Jamie was reasonable. "Relax, Tyler, Kayla will save you. Call her."

Tyler went instantly to his phone and called Kayla.

"Kayla Davie."

"I'm in one hell of a bind—"

"Tyler?"

"Yeah. You're the only one to save me. You *have* to be at our place by eight-thirty tonight. Of all the things I've—"

"I can't possibly be there tonight. I have a class this evening."

No date? And he said, "You do remember Barbara Nelson." It wasn't even a question. He immediately went on, "She's coming to our place tonight between nine and ten to get a brief I've been working on."

"You went over the deadline?"

"You know better. This is almost a month too soon."

Kayla asked, "How much work do you still have to do on it?"

"Not much. And I can do a final on the computer at our place."

"It is not 'our' place," Kayla reminded her ex. "We're divorced."

Turning his back to Jamie, Tyler said to Kayla in a low, hushed voice, "I never sleep on your half of the bed."

"You need to spread your wings and fly. You're free."

"No." Then he cleared his suddenly clogged throat and begged, "Just tonight. Please."

Kayla sighed with great impatience and made mouth noises of resistance.

Holding the phone to his ear, Tyler was silent.

She said, "I'll *try* to be there by nine. Tyler, you're a grown man. No woman can intimidate you. Barbara is a pushover. Just say *no!*"

"'No!' doesn't always work."

With some droll irony, Kayla commented, "I'm aware of that. I can't believe *any* woman could rattle you. How come Barbara can? She's harmless!"

Harmless! He urged in a low, very serious voice, "Be there. Please. Be sure to come. I really need you there. And for Pete's sake, don't delay until after nine."

"What happens at nine?"

"I can only speculate with terror."

The heartless Kayla laughed as she hung up.

Slowly, Tyler put his phone back in its cradle. He sat quietly, looking very serious.

Jamie soothed, "There'll be no problem. You'll manage. You're a logical, arguing male, and you have that additional talent of being physically strong."

"I cannot clip a woman on the jaw."

"Oh."

Tyler turned his chair so that he faced Jamie. "You have no problem with that?"

Jamie shrugged and turned his hands palm up. "No woman has ever attacked me. I look on you as a sun god whom women adore."

Tyler said several words any really tough sailor would have envied.

"Where'd you learn those?" Jamie asked with respect.

And Tyler told Jamie where to go—how, in such colorful language, that Jamie was awed. He exclaimed, "Wait! Let me write that down! Wow." And Jamie whistled softly in admiration.

Tyler sagged in his chair. He put a hand to his forehead just right and said, "See? Just *see* what Miss Nelson has done to a good young man? I haven't said any of those words since I was seventeen and my daddy wrestled me down and made me lick a bar of soap."

"Wow! He must'a been something to've wrestled you down."

"My mother was there with a shotgun and told me if I touched one hair on him that she'd shoot me."

"What all had you done, for Pete's sake." An unquestioning statement that encourages confidences.

In a deadly voice, Tyler told Jamie, "You're too young to hear it all."

"But you minded your fragile momma."

"She had a gun."

"She wouldn't-a killed her precious son."

"You need to know Momma better. She only *looks* like a lady."

Jamie turned out his hand. "She acts like one."

Tyler nodded. "You know her. You've met her. You've observed her. She *seems* to be a lady." Tyler shook his head. "It's facade. She's a killer. She loves my daddy." Tyler considered in a black, brooding way, before he said thoughtfully, "He probably deserves it."

And Jamie laughed.

It was only then that Tyler realized, all that while, Jamie had had his chair turned and he was facing Tyler and watching him. It was a serious first. Tyler actually had all of Jamie's attention.

Tyler asked an older, hopefully wiser man, "What'll I do if Kayla can't make it tonight?"

"Lie down, close your eyes and think of England?" Jamie had some English blood and he knew that was what mothers told virginal daughters for their wedding night.

But Tyler scoffed. "America has more problems than England."

Jamie explained, "It was an old saying of solving something beyond you."

"I'll remember it. But I won't be thinking of England."

"No? What?"

Through his teeth, Tyler enunciated, "Revenge."

"Wow!"

"'The time has come,' the Walrus said, 'to speak of many things—'"

Jamie laughed. "So. What do you want to talk about?"

And Tyler said seriously, "You cotton to that Nelson terror. Why not consider an invasion."

Then oddly, tellingly, Jamie cautioned, "Careful."

The one word caused both men to be silent and very serious. Jamie was Miss Nelson's protector. She didn't yet realize it. She might never. But right then, Jamie was telling Tyler to watch his mouthiness. Interesting.

Finally, Tyler asked, "Are you sure you care for

her that much?'' And there was such doubt in Tyler's soft words.

Jamie just jerked his head down once in a positive nod of commitment. His stern eyes never left Tyler's.

Slowly, a twinkle began in Tyler's eyes, and he began to smile. He said, "When she attacks me, I'll tell her I'm your loyal friend, and you love her."

"Behave."

In irritation, Tyler complained, "Why don't you tell *her* that?"

In a steely voice, Jamie said, "I'm counting on you to be a gentleman and behave yourself."

Tyler dramatically threw up his arms and groused, "If I was a woman I could file a complaint, and Miss Nelson would be forced to back off."

"You can file such a complaint, now, as a man— but I warn you that such a filing would harm Barb." He paused and narrowed his eyes. In a soft, deadly voice Jamie told Tyler, "I wouldn't like that."

"Why don't you just go up to her and say, 'Leave Tyler alone. I'm willing.' That would solve all of my problems except Kayla and I'm working on her."

And Jamie had the gall to put in, "Why don't you give up and leave Kayla alone?"

Tyler sighed with great drama and looked aside. "She loves me."

Jamie snorted. "You need to confront reality. She accepted it that you divorced her. That ought to be some sort of clue for you, right there."

"Quit being so negative."

Jamie silently watched Tyler for a while, then he moved his body to guide his chair back to his desk. There, he was immediately involved with the papers on his desk.

Tyler thought what a good lawyer Jamie was. When he split from the firm, he would ask Jamie if he could go along with him.

Would Jamie agree? That would be interesting to know.

Back to his own papers, Tyler sighed deeply with some quiet drama. Kayla was a nuisance. He glanced at the window. It was fake. Their office was in the center of the building. No windows. To have windows, one had to have clout. Neither he nor Jamie had any clout.

No client was ever in the firm's offices. Any interview was in one of the conference rooms at the table there.

Tyler and Jamie had pooled their money and bought the fake window. It had been a nine-day wonder. None of the other associates had had the nerve to buy their own pull-down, sheet window.

There were stick'ems to put on the shade. Tiny people who were walking down the fake street. One had to look closely to see them. The stick'ems Tyler and Jamie used were string covered bathing beauties walking barefooted on the city street.

Almost right away and standing, the two had listened to Miss Nelson's lecture. The two did that silently but with total attention. Tyler tended to be argumentative, but Jamie stopped that with one deadly look as Tyler opened his mouth for his first intake of breath.

After Miss Nelson told them the string swimsuits were unsuitable for a law office in the middle of San Antonio, Tyler found stick'em clothed people who happened to be markedly female. Not one male.

With Miss Nelson's distaste—jealousy?—of the strings covered, barefooted city walkers in the fake window, Jamie would have discarded the entire window. It was Tyler whose independence was challenged.

As Tyler sighed, Jamie suggested, "Maybe Kayla objected to your hard nosed, dictatorial manner?"

Tyler said, "No. She loves me."

"So *that's* why she left!"

"No." Tyler picked up a pencil and examined it. But then he went on, "We stumbled on a gathering and went to see what was happening. It was a pit fight between dogs. I'd never seen such and wanted a look. While I was doing that, she bought four of the dogs, put them in my car and left. I walked home."

"Were you angry?"

"By the time I got home, I was no longer ticked. She was asleep in our bed. The dogs were all around her. They just looked at me, very alert, with softly threatening throat growls. They didn't want her wakened. I decided to sleep on the couch."

When Jamie quit laughing, Tyler continued, "When I woke up the next morning, she was gone. If the dogs had still been there, I would've thought they'd eaten her. But she and all those dogs had disappeared. She never did apologize."

"Apologize to *you*? Are you that stupid? You've never given one clue to being such a stupid man!"

"I was wrong?"

"Don't you realize that?"

"Why...no. When I stumbled into the dogfight, I looked. I'd never seen one before then. I thought she'd be as interested because she'd never been to one, either."

"Did she want to see one?"

Tyler was logical. "We were surprised."

"I guess you were! How could you have been so—insensitive?"

Tyler spread his arms. "If you don't know how people live, how can you judge them?"

"I can agree to that—to a degree. She isn't a lawyer. She wouldn't try any cases on dogfights or murder. She didn't *need* to see a dogfight."

Being a lawyer, Tyler argued, "There were women there who were excited and yelling and betting."

"It takes all kinds—" Jamie threw in that old saw.

Earnestly, Tyler communicated, "I'd rather go to a dogfight than to have Miss Nelson come to my place. Are you *sure* you can't be there tonight?"

"If there was any way, at all, that I could come and help Barb past you, I would. Could you possibly make it another night?"

"This wasn't my doing! I told you that. She just—arranged it. She terrifies me."

"When Barb finally realizes what a gem I am, and we marry, I may hesitate to have you as best man."

"I don't believe I could be a part of that sacrifice of a friend marrying that woman."

With serious, narrowed eyes, Jamie said, "I told you to be careful."

Tyler lifted his hands in surrender, but his mouth said, "Don't do anything that rash. If you're ever tempted, let me get a bunch to talk you through it."

"Be quiet." And Jamie went back to his computer. He was through talking.

Tyler considered his office mate. This was the longest conversation they'd ever had. And Jamie hadn't been reading papers or shifting them at the time. He'd given his whole, entire attention to Tyler.

And being attracted by the Nelson witch, Jamie had not once gotten hot or angry. He'd not once lost his temper. He'd warned Tyler firmly, but with neutral words, no swearing, and his comments about Miss Nelson were kind.

Hmmm.

Tyler's mind looked at Miss Nelson to see what Jamie could possibly see in such a harpy. But, as Tyler considered their legal supervisor, his mouth was sour. And he sighed. He was going to have to save Jamie from that woman. With Jamie so positive and firm about her, it wasn't going to be easy to make him understand.

But there was no way, at *all,* that Tyler was going to throw his own body at the lioness just to save Jamie. No way. Nuh-uh. Not that. There were limits even in friendship.

With that acknowledgment, Tyler buckled down and there was relative quiet in the office. The females on the window were frozen in the silent time that passed in the busyness of the office. The phones rang. People talked in the hallway. Doors opened and closed.

Neither lawyer heard those things. Their ears were selective. Their minds could concentrate.

It was almost five-thirty before Tyler was ready to leave his office. The brief was finished. He only needed to smooth the indicated wording on his own computer and print out a fresh copy. It would be ready when Miss Nelson came for it.

He called Kayla.

He got her just before she left her office. He talked fast and serious, going over the same crisis so that she would understand.

Again she impatiently agreed several times.

He finished earnestly, "Be there."

"I *told* you that I would!" And she hung up the phone.

She wasn't even courteous. No wonder he'd divorced her.

Tyler was so upset by that Nelson woman that he couldn't eat much for supper. He had to throw away the peanut butter sandwich. His mouth was too dry to eat peanut butter.

How could a divorced man who was twenty-eight years old be intimidated by any woman?

At his apartment, Tyler finished the brief and verified it was accurate, neat and tidy. He lay it carefully on the dining-room table. It was in the one cleared space in the accumulated clutter of mail, books and papers.

Then, in dread of Miss Nelson, he paced. Time passed. Kayla didn't arrive ahead of Miss Nelson. The threat of being alone with such a barracuda scared Tyler's stomach.

Miss Nelson came early, at a quarter of nine. She smiled a friendly smile as she mentioned, "It's been a hairy day."

Tyler was all business. He went directly to the brief in its protective folder, picked it up, turned and found Miss Nelson right in front of him. He stepped one long step back and held the folder out to Miss Nelson.

She put her purse on the table and the table held firm with the added weight. Kayla had chosen that table. It was a good one. Too bad. If it had crashed under the additional weight of Miss Nelson's purse, she might have left in a flurry. Unfortunately, the table held.

Miss Nelson said to the silent Tyler, "It's been a bearcat of a day."

Tyler held the folder in front of him, ready for her to take it. He had no conversation to share. None at all. He lifted the folder a third time. Third time charm. It would work. She would take it. And she would leave.

Sure.

As he had dreaded, Miss Nelson inquired with a slight smile. "Do you have a beer? Any wine?"

"I don't believe so."

"Don't be so selfish," she said over her shoulder as she turned and walked into the kitchen.

Tyler stood, undecided. Should he follow her? She might consider that friendly. If he stayed out of the kitchen, she might feel she was intruding.

From the kitchen came the immediate exclamation, "What a *mess!*"

Tyler frowned and went to the kitchen door. Annoyed, he looked around. Then he snapped, "You should have seen it before I cleaned it up!" He wasn't being funny. His tone rode on indignation.

And the front door opened!

Kayla was there!

Tyler started for her as he exclaimed, "You're here!"

She hissed, "Stay away from me. My car wouldn't start. I had to take a cab here."

And Tyler thought how different the two women were. They ought to switch attitudes.

And just as Kayla asked, "I thought the witch would be heee—" Miss Nelson came through the kitchen door.

Having heard Kayla's comment, Miss Nelson smiled. She was a woman who wasn't where she was because of timidity. She said, "You must be Kayla."

Kayla nodded. "I'm a Davie."

That altered Miss Nelson's attitude. She asked, "Which line?"

And Kayla replied, "My daddy is Paul."

"Ah."

Whatever that meant.

"So your sister is Lauren." Miss Nelson wasn't questioning.

And Kayla replied, "Of course."

"Kyle Phillips just married her."

It hadn't been very long ago that Kayla's sister, Lauren, had spent a freak, three-day snowstorm alone with Kyle...at his place. How interesting that this woman mentioned it.

Kayla gave a shiveringly cool look at Miss Nelson. "You have some problem with that?" Being a Davie helped.

"Of course not."

"Were you invited to the wedding?"

"No."

"How strange you brought up the subject." Then Kayla looked at Tyler with deliberately opened eyes. "Will this take any more time?"

"Not long," Tyler said very kindly. "We just have to go over a brief to be sure I did it right. I know you're tired. Curl up, here, on the sofa. We'll soon be done."

Kayla looked briefly at the mess piled up on the

dining-room table and flinched. She closed her eyes in discipline, then went into the living room where she removed the magazines and papers before she curled up on the sofa.

The drapes were open. Tyler hadn't wanted to be—enclosed—with Miss Nelson. With the drapes open, at least someone could have seen inside. That fact might have prevented Miss Nelson's assault on him if Kayla hadn't made it there in time.

But Kayla was there.

At the portion of the dining-room table that Tyler had cleared, Miss Nelson was seated. She moved over so that Tyler could sit next to her, but he sat on the opposite side of the table. He said, "I have the file copy."

She said, "Be sure it's returned tomorrow."

And he replied, "Yes'um."

She asked, "Is—Kayla spending the night?"

That question scared the hairs on his arms and up his spine. He replied, "We're divorced." It was not really any kind of reply.

That was the first time Tyler had ever admitted aloud to her that they were that word...divorced.

Miss Nelson proceeded to read. But his saying that he was half of a divorce had silenced Tyler and sent him into a strange vacuum. His ears popped with the silence. It was very strange. He was divorced. He was no longer half of a pair. He really was divorced.

He turned and looked at the couch beyond in the living room. He could see the dark hair of the other half of their divorce. Her hair was puffed over the arm of the couch. She was lying down, resting. And he thought of seeing her lying down and looking up at him.

As the unaware Miss Nelson read the brief, across the mess of the table, her host was remembering his wife naked and close to him. She'd smiled and licked her lips, lifting her mouth to his.

Erotic imaginings were not unknown, especially with a man whose wife has deserted him. But it was a little strange for Tyler to be dreaming erotica concerning his ex-wife when there was a distastefully interested woman across the table from him. Why erotica? Why now?

It was because of his wife's long, dark hair that bunched under her head and was visible over the arm of the sofa in the next room. The back of the sofa blocked seeing the rest of Kayla. Only her puffed, dark hair was visible. That soft mass that lured Tyler's attention and slithered erotica into his brain...his senses...his neglected sex.

Four

With Miss Nelson across the table, reading quietly, Tyler relaxed minimally. He heard Kayla yawn and the small sounds of her unseen body settling on the sofa. He glanced at Miss Nelson. Had she heard? Kayla was there for the stretch of time Miss Nelson would stay.

Something warm stirred in Tyler's heart. It was stupidity. Kayla no longer loved him. She was being staunch for a past commitment. That was a Davie trait. Once committed, they stood by their word.

But it was only honor. Kayla no longer loved Tyler. However reluctant, she just felt duty bound to aid him in a crisis.

Tyler's phenomenal eyelashes lowered to shield his sad eyes. Kayla. His wife…no longer. But she *had* come there to be his shield. She had done that.

The silence crackled in tiny ear pops. He could hear

the Nelson woman's breathing. The sound of it was
hungry and taught. She wanted Tyler's body. He was
glad Kayla was there.

And Tyler considered women who are vulnerable
to physically stronger men. He thought he just might
take up the Women's Cause. He could be an advocate
for women's freedom. They'd be grateful, and he'd
have to list times when each could have him alone.

He'd give Kayla first choice.

Just watch, she'd wave a hand spread in front of
her and say, "Never mind."

Her body wasn't as greedy as other women's. Like
Barbara Nelson's. An avaricious double greed. What
made that Nelson woman act like a man? Like a hunting man who used and discarded.

And Barbara's husky voice said softly, "You do a
wonderful job of it."

The very words terrified Tyler. He gasped and—

Barbara went on, "This brief is perfectly done.
Thank you."

Seriously, he replied, "You're welcome."

Regretfully, Barbara glanced over at the dark hair
visible over the arm of the couch. "It's too bad we
can't visit now." She did hesitate for his reply, but
with his silence, Barbara went on, "We'd probably
waken her." She gestured to the back of the sofa and
the dark hair that could be seen.

Tyler continued silent.

So Barbara asked, "Or would you like me to help
you waken her so that she could leave? It must be a
burden when an ex-wife just wanders in on you."

Tyler didn't reply.

Barbara sighed. "It must be difficult for a man your

age to have the problem of an ex-wife who doesn't know better than to hang around."

Thinking of his strident effort in getting Kayla there, Tyler continued his silence.

"You are loyal." Barbara was somewhat droll. "I'll take this along." She smiled. "See you tomorrow."

He nodded once. He stood rigidly alert. He was breathing high in his chest. He had escaped the vulture's talons? He walked over to the door and opened it, tensely holding it open.

Barbara gathered her things thoughtfully, making noises and dropped one large book that should have lifted the sleeping beauty right off the sofa. To the wakeful couple, the continued silence from the sofa was a surprise. Neither commented.

Tyler had opened the door all the way back against the wall, so there was no hindrance at *all* in Barbara's move to the front door. She paused and smiled at Tyler.

His face was serious.

Barbara said, "Another time."

He only looked at her with distanced seriousness. He made no reply.

His supervisor then moved through the door, and he gently closed it after her. He pressed against the door and heard the bolt lock. He was safe.

He turned to look at his ex-wife, but his eyes moved sideways and looked beyond. The drapes had been left open. He could see into the street. He didn't move. He saw Barbara after she had emerged from the building.

She glanced up at his window.

He stood as he was, facing the couch but watching sideways through his thick lashes.

Barbara went to her car and got in. But she didn't start it. She watched his window.

From the couch, Kayla asked through stiff lips, "Is she gone?"

Through unmoving lips he replied, "Don't move. The drapes are open. Her car is still there. She's watching to see if you'll leave. If you do, she'll come back here!"

With a still face, Kayla managed, "Oh, for Pete's sake!"

Equally careful, he replied urgently, "Don't let her see you're awake. She'll come back!"

"This is ridiculous."

"I agree. I find I'm quite compassionate with women's rights. I'll probably volunteer to help them with their cause!"

"Well, that's a plus."

"I always treated you as an individual."

"You treated me as if I was an iron-stomached man!"

Without moving his lips, he managed to exclaim, "I did not!"

"You took me to the tackiest places!"

"I thought you'd appreciate the fact I was expanding your awareness!"

"Close the drapes so I can sit up and argue."

He declined. "She needs to think we're here for the night. I'll come over and carry you to the bedroom, turning out—"

"No you don't." How could she be that positive without moving?

He assured her, "It's for *effect!* Quit thinking I'm just trying to get inside your underwear!"

She was silent. He tidied up the room, crossing in front of the open drapes. Then he went and squatted down beside his ex-wife. Slowly, carefully, he put back her hair and lay his hand on her head softly as if he was admiring her. Since his back was then to the window, he could quite easily tell her, "I'm going to carry you into the other room. She'll think you're spending the night. A sort of old home time. Pretend you're still asleep. Be lax."

"I think this is some sort of trap. Is she *really* out there?"

"Yep. When I pick you up, you put your chin on my shoulder. Then you can peek across my back and you'll see her car on the corner across the intersection. It's the first one parked on the west side of the street there."

"I'm to be lax and pretend deep sleep?"

"Please."

"You're a big nuisance."

"I'm worth saving."

"From...her?"

"She's a barracuda."

"She must be desperate if she's trying for you."

Sarcastic, he labeled her comment. "Thanks."

"Anytime. Tell me when you plan to lift me. I'll try to help."

"Don't. You have to look lax and asleep."

"Don't drop me."

He chided softly, "I never have."

"The other times you carried me, I helped."

"I've been working out...my frustrations."

"At the gym or with what's-her-face?"

He almost smiled. "You curious?"

"No. I'm bored. This has been a real drag. In that long silence, I just about sat up and peeked over the back of the sofa."

He inquired, "Why? To see if we were there?"

"To see if I could slip away."

"Oh." Then, still squatted down, he said, "I'm gonna get you."

And she asked instantly, "What's that mean?"

As he carefully seemed to push her hair back, he innocently assured her, "I just meant it's time for me to scoop you up and carry you out of sight."

"Don't stumble."

He chided, his voice in his deep throat, "Have I ever?"

Again, she reminded him, "I always helped."

He offered, "I can put your arm around my neck."

"My left one."

He questioned with interest, "Not both?"

"If you try to put my right arm up, you might break my arm."

He scoffed, "Ah, ye of little faith."

"If you don't want me to sink my teeth into your throat, be careful."

He was somewhat surprised. "You've joined some bat group?"

"No. It's self-protection."

So he eased his arms under her unresisting body and picked her up. As he stood, it was with some effort. She flopped her head with the movement and peeked beyond the window. She muttered, "She's there, all right, and watching. How nosy of her."

"Hush."

He moved, her head slid sideways and her body appeared to adjust itself as a limp burden.

He commented, "You've gained some weight."

As he walked around the end of the sofa, her indignant, hidden mouth said, "I have not! It's because I'm not helping! That's all! Shall I put my arms up on your shoulders and help? How *dare* you say I'm heavy!"

He began to smother his laugh. He stopped at the light switch and turned off the living-room lights. He was in the lighted hallway. He stood quietly, his head tilted down as if he was cherishing the sight of her.

She said, "Let's get this over with. Quit stalling."

He leaned his head down and kissed her mouth.

She *almost* burst from him. He felt that first rejection, but she stayed limp!

Her lips softened.

When he lifted his mouth from hers, she was still limp. She said, "You dirty rat."

And he replied, "I know."

"How mature of you to realize that you're wicked and nasty."

Again, he said, "I know." He walked on into the bedroom and asked, "Is it any different?"

"I don't suppose you've washed the sheets since I left."

"Try them." He lay her on the bed with great care. "Familiar?"

She moved, wiggling away from his grasp. "You can let up, she can't see us here."

"Well, she's still there. I haven't heard her start the car. You've got to stay here until she leaves. Remember what all I did to discourage Miles?"

"That was a long time ago…before we were married."

"But you were glad I stayed around, and he finally left."

"Yes."

"Stay with me, now."

"I *am!*" she said with impatience. "I've been here this whole evening! It wasn't necessary!"

"You have to've heard what she said when she left."

"Yes. I did. She was after you. Things at the office must be pretty dull if that old bag is after somebody as young as you."

He was calm and logical. "I'm a mature male." How strange to feel adult with her and not as much so with Miss Nelson. He mused on the difference.

But Kayla was replying to his comment of being mature. She finished his sentence with, "—for someone younger than she."

"Would you mind if I looked for another woman?"

"Who?" How betraying! Why had her tongue said that? Kayla then asked, "Who did you have in mind? Not that old biddy?" Why couldn't she resist calling attention to Barbara being older? It was probably because there was such a gap in their ages.

But then Kayla wondered if she could use age as a block for Tyler if he was interested in a woman younger than he? Or…younger…than she? Why should she care? She did not. It was only that she had once been committed to him, and she had not yet entirely resolved that commitment.

Tyler slowly paced the room while Kayla stacked the pillows behind her on the bed. She watched him.

He was beautifully made. He moved like a panther. His eyes were the calm threat of such a beast.

He said, "It's time, now, to turn off these lights."

"No."

"You have the bed. I'll not get into it with you. I'll sit over here. But we should turn off the lights."

Considering their observer, it would be correct to turn off the lights. She suggested, "We're separated, divorced." She'd added that word with some acknowledgment. "Leave the lights on. To her, we could be curious about each other and—doing it—in the light."

His voice was kind and logical. "We've had enough time to do it leisurely. Any other couple would have been at it right away and hungry. We've had the time to be slow and easy." And he added soberly, "It's time to turn out the lights."

"We could be talking?"

"We'd be exhausted."

She couldn't hush up. She said, "I remember—" And she stopped abruptly.

He waited. "What is it you remember?" And his voice was soft and kind.

She looked up at him and told him, "I've forgotten what I was going to say. I suppose we ought to turn out the lights."

"I'll do that. That way I can check the living-room window and see if Miss Nelson is still watching."

"Good idea." Then she mentioned, "You call her—Miss Nelson."

"I try to distance us in age."

"Distance. You—or—her?"

"I try to call the age difference to her mind."

Of course, that set Kayla off in laughter.

He turned off the lights, and she still laughed. Then he moved like a shadow and went into the living room. That silenced Kayla. Tyler was still a while, then he came back into the bedroom. "She's still there."

He lied.

With the lights off, Kayla didn't even consider that he could be clever and lie. That was odd for her, but she was so honest that it didn't occur to her that Tyler might be underhanded.

He said, "Settle down and rest. I'll stay over here on the chair."

"Uh—"

She'd been ready to suggest that she sneak out the back door to the utility room and hail a cab or catch the bus.

He said, "I'll take good care of you."

Kayla thought it was just a good thing she'd told Henrietta, her apartment mate who had cats, that she might be late getting home. Then she'd told Hennie why she was going out. The excuse covered her for the entire night.

The entire night?

That was…an alluring idea.

She moved on the bed's rustling sheets. With subtle sounds, she yawned and then she sighed, very softly. Sadly.

Tyler hesitated. She moved like a snake, slowly, and her sighs were quietly deep. It didn't sound restless. None of it. She sounded as if she wanted him over on the bed with her, on her, in her.

His own breathing picked up.

She could hear that. He was breathing high in his chest. He was triggered. He'd always been easy.

She took her time turning over and moving subtly. He thought her movements were as if she was silently restless. Wanting. Wanting him.

He was willing. Man, was he willing! He moved to the bed. His shirt became unbuttoned. But the zipper on his trousers did make an ear-catching sound. And he shed them with whispers of cloth being moved.

He could have been pulling up a light blanket, but it was his trousers that were discarded. He eased down on the side of the bed like a dog that isn't sure he's allowed inside the house. His breathing was a little harsh.

He'd be easy. She smiled in the night.

But the scarce light caught the fact that her eyes glinted, and she was betrayed to him as willing.

With her willing and calling attention to herself, he left the room and checked out the absent woman who had left some time before.

He returned to the bedroom, and she asked, "Still there?"

And he replied, "I wonder if she ever sleeps." A nothing reply.

Kayla sighed with great endurance. "Know any good jokes? Any gossip? With the light out, you need to entertain me. Of course, I *could* leave—soon—and walk along carefully until I got a cab and could sit with gentleness."

"I'd rather you stay. She might take even your careful leaving as a sign I was again alone...and vulnerable."

"This is a drag."

"I'll distract you."

"How?"

Ah. So he had some time and teasing and tasting to do first...if he could discipline himself enough. He'd endured a long dry spell. He asked her, "All the lechers been buzzing around you?"

She replied, "You're the only lecher I know."

"How about Jack?"

"Not Jack."

"What about Ray?"

"No."

"Who?"

"Nobody."

"You looking around, trying for guys?"

"No."

Carefully, he said the words softly, "You want—me." She moved on the bed. The darkness of the room shadowed her. But his adjusted vision saw that she had discarded her skirt and blouse. Again, he said, "You want me."

"No."

"Yes. You want me. You're teasing me with taking off your clothes."

She gasped quite well and protested, "I'd forgotten your cat eyes! How could I have forgotten you can see in the dark! You lecher! A woman isn't ever safe with you!"

"Do you...want to be safe?"

She tilted her chin. "Of course."

"How safe?"

She put the tip of her finger on her lower lip and considered. "Why are you on the bed?"

"I've had a long day. Protecting you from that harpy has exhausted me. I need to lie down for a while. Talk to me so I can forget the harassment of the day.''

''Who all harassed you?''

''You saw the primary one. She terrifies me.''

''A man like you, with your sexual talents, can cope with a needy woman.''

''No.''

''It's easy.''

''I'm a one-woman man. You're the woman.''

She laughed. Genuinely amused and pleased for his words. She believed him.

In a soft, rather roughened, low voice, he then told her, ''It's been so long, I've forgotten how.''

That made her really laugh. She put her hand to her face and pretended to hide the laughter. She was not successful. Just her sounds stirred him further.

He shifted closer, but she moved to the side of the bed. She said, ''I need to see if the vampire is still there.''

Tyler gasped almost silently and he did reach for her, but she slithered out of the bed and was gone.

He lay back, defeated. Of course, he could be surprised that Miss Nelson had finally left.

Kayla came back to the bed and told him, ''She's still there! Can I leave by the back door?''

He was riveted! Kayla had lied. Or had the harpy come back? Why would Miss Nelson leave for all that time and then return? She was not there! Kayla wanted to taunt him. She wanted to test him!

He patted the bed beside him and said, ''It's too late for a cab. I'll take you home later. You might as well lie down and be comfortable.''

His arm slid under her shoulders and he pulled her closer to him. He said, ''It's been so long—''

He kissed her.

While her body was flacid, her soft mouth was hungry.

That shot the trigger and his breathing accelerated considerably. Her body was malleable. Her body was hungry for *him!*

His laugh was low in his throat and curled her toes. His kiss then was wicked and his hand moved… wonderfully.

She muttered and breathed and squirmed for him to get closer. Her breaths almost matched his. She moaned and moved and pulled at him.

He loved it. He loved her.

She said, "I'm in a free time, you don't need the condom."

"You're sure?"

"I never take a risk."

But he stopped, breathed, and got the sheath.

That was probably a good thing, because, then, they could take a little more time and pleasure.

A woman was a woman. How strange that he could not even consider one and was impotent to her charms, but Kayla set him off like a shooting star.

And she did just exactly that.

She gasped and her hands held him closer. She made relishing sounds and she was like a wild woman. She rushed him along the fast winds to the zenith, and they made it together. They held for the rapture and slowly collapsed.

He lay replete with his forearms holding most of his weight as he recovered enough to move his weight somewhat from her perfect, fragile, inert body.

He asked, "Are you all right?"

She rubbed her hands on his back and said, "Ummmmmmmmm."

He laughed softly in his throat.

Eventually, he managed to lift his body to one side and lie on his back, sundered, his hand holding hers, his other arm over his face like a done man.

The silence was healing. Tyler knew they'd finally crossed back to being a couple. They'd—

And Kayla said, "If we walked out now, she'd probably follow."

He asked slowly, rejecting moving anywhere at all, "What would Hennie say if you took me to bed at your place? No, no. I could not *dare* to leave your place alone. That woman would track me down."

Thoughtfully, Kayla was silent. Then she said with decision, "We have to find Barbara a man of her own."

"Jamie loves her."

"Jamie! I'd always thought Jamie was an intelligent man!"

"He is, but he has this one flaw. He thinks that woman is perfect."

"How could he possibly be so hoodwinked? You need to talk to him."

"He won't allow it. I've tried. But Jamie is staunch and faithful and zonked." He was silent. Then he added, "She calls him 'Johnny.'"

"The woman's blind and stupid."

"She's a brilliant lawyer," Tyler admitted. But then he added, "But she has serious flaws."

In the dark, Kayla questioned, "Flaws?" She considered the word. Then she told him softly, "You have a few."

And he replied earnestly, "I'm young enough to be retrained...by a caring woman."

And just like that, Kayla said quickly, "I agree, but I really think you ought to keep away from Barbara."

Tyler drew a slow, patient breath and told her, "I was referring to you." He grinned, his eyes sleepy.

She shocked him wide-awake. "There are just things one person cannot do for another. In the time we were married, I didn't even dent you. I—"

"I dented you."

"Don't be vulgar. You know full well what I mean. I've never in my life known such an underlife as you dragged me to see."

He gestured earnestly and his reply was serious, "But look at what you learned! Why else would you have gotten on the Animal Protection League? You've been a godsend for them. You're relentless with it. Look at the laws you've managed to get noticed. Would you have done all that if you hadn't been to the places I showed you?"

"When we discovered the pit fights, you weren't looking for animal rights."

She was partially right. He had taken her to odd places to expand her. He retorted, "I've never seen any woman who was as cosseted as you've been. Your daddy carried his daughters on silk cushions."

"With the weird places you took me, if the effort had been to jolt me, you were successful. I was jolted."

They lay silent and brooding. How could he get back her love when she thought he was a tacky man? He needed a break. He said, "I'll check and see if she's left."

"Uhhh—"

He hesitated and turned to look at her. She was very serious and her eyes on him were big and somehow sad or disappointed.

She said, "Okay." Her voice was soft.

He went to the living room door and looked across the room and out that window. As he'd known, Barbara's car was long gone.

He scrunched his mouth in defeat. Kayla could leave. He turned back to his room, and she was right in front of him.

She peeked around the doorjamb. "Is she—? She's gone."

He stood watching her carefully sober eyes. She was wondering if he knew that she'd lied in order to stay with him and test his restraint. Women do that.

He looked down at his ex-wife standing there naked. All her clothes were gone.

Actually, so was she. She was there, but she wasn't his wife anymore. She no longer loved him. She had allowed him the surcease of her body, but it was diminishing for him to be such a supplicant.

Instead of groveling, he should refrain. It was a matter of his feeling of self-worth.

He said kindly, "I'll take you home."

In the same room, in the dark, silently, the two found their discarded clothing and dressed. Each was unhappy.

Tyler said, "I'll go start the car. Just pull the door to. I have the keys." And he left the apartment.

Kayla stood still for a minute and frowned. She slowly finished her dressing.

So when she got into Tyler's car, Kayla said, "I've spoken with Hennie, I'm going home tonight."

He only nodded. The Davie conduct was never predictable.

Tyler drove with skill. The two no-longer-marrieds were silent. They had nothing to communicate.

The traffic wasn't heavy at that time of night. San Antonio was like any other city. There was a nightlife, but it wasn't as traffic heavy as the busy day lives.

They went out Broadway to Alamo Heights to one of the big old houses there. It was the Davie house and had been in the family for over a hundred years. The yard was well done, the house was pristine, the oaks were trimmed of the nasty, sap sucking moss balls which look like baby porcupines.

Kayla said, "You'll have to come in. It would be rude of you not to say hello."

So Tyler got out of the car and took a deep breath. The Davie bunch was a little off kilter.

The legally divorced, emotionally separated couple went into the big house. And in the television room sat Goldilocks, the Davie Cook.

Cook was her title. She ran the whole shebang and all the people even remotely attached to the place. She knew *everything*.

Goldilocks eyed Tyler and groused, "'bout time you came along."

"Hello, yourself."

"How come you brought her here?"

Kayla said, "Now, Goldi—"

"I ain't talkin' to you, chile. Hush."

Kayla turned to Tyler and commented, "If you will recall, she takes this attitude whenever she's nosy. She speaks perfectly well on other occasions."

"I tole you to hush yo mouth."

"I will."

"Now."

"Yes'um."

"Sit down, Tyler, and tell me wha-chur doin'."

"I wouldn't interrupt your TV. Good to see you, Goldi—"

"Hush up and sit down."

As with everybody else, he did as Goldilocks directed. Tyler was amused. He'd never had to buckle under for anybody else, but with Goldilocks, it just seemed obligatory. She spoke. The object obeyed.

He was an object.

Five

Goldilocks sat there on a soft chair which was *hers*. Anybody that sat in it risked a horrific death! She wore a long, loose, boldly patterned, cotton gown with short bat sleeves. Her head was wrapped in a purple cloth. She was striking.

She was the envy of all who saw her. Not many women had the élan to wear such dramatic dress. Goldilocks had the drama. She looked like a visiting Queen of some distant place, maybe not on this planet.

When she had arrived, about eighteen years before, she had almost immediately taken over the entire Davie household, and since then, she had ruled. She knew every member of the extended Davie family, who they were, how they behaved, what they owned, how they lived and every single scandal.

On occasion, Kayla's mother would chide Goldilocks with something like, "She's a fifth cousin!"

And Goldilocks would mention aloofly, "She's no real kin to *you* at all." As if being a wife was an intrusion, but Goldilocks was family.

That attitude did tick Kayla's mother.

From the very beginning, Goldilocks had accepted membership in the Davie family, but she would remind the head's *wife* that she was an intruder by marriage.

So, being in charge, Goldilocks grilled Kayla's ex-husband. That was interesting to any lawyer...being grilled. Tyler was vastly amused...but only inside his head. He gave Goldilocks his attention. He talked readily, but he never told anything. He replied without ever revealing a thing.

A lot of lawyers are like that. They appear so interested and cooperative, so kind and courteous. So helpful. But they are completely locked up. They never allow anything to actually be revealed. Age, place of birth—nothing.

Of course, Goldilocks already knew all that about Tyler from Kayla. But she never pried anything else out of Tyler. She watched his eyes and never saw a flicker of thought or a flinch at a question. He was so—earnest. The damned tight-lipped, stuffed headed snot.

But worse, *he* asked innocent questions, in turn.

Goldilocks just about spilled her guts, until she realized what he was doing, and she shut up entirely. She told him to be quiet or run along home.

He was shocked. Beautifully, subtly offended.

Goldilocks apologized. She did!

That left Kayla speechless for the first time in her entire life!

So after Tyler accepted the apology, and even got up and kissed Goldilock's cheek, the woman was so rattled for the first time in her whole life, that she got up, excused herself and sailed off to her room.

Awed, Kayla asked in a whisper, "How'd you manage that?"

And he replied casually, "I'm a good lawyer."

"If you can handle Goldilocks, you must be able to wither Barbara. Why does she rattle you?"

"She isn't Goldilocks." Then he looked over at Kayla very seriously as he added, "Neither are you."

"You are mistaken, if you think for one minute that I can control Goldilocks the way you just did when she was grilling you."

"You and Barbara baffle me. I don't know how to handle either of you."

"Ask Goldilocks."

He looked over at her quickly, vulnerably.

Kayla hastened to add, "—about Barbara."

So Tyler rose from his chair and went down the hallway to the closed door of Goldilocks's room. But she declined to acknowledge his tap.

Tyler sent Goldilocks roses the next day. She pitched them.

With hot fury, Kayla retrieved them from the trash.

Goldilocks tilted back her head and just watched Kayla over her cheekbones. That didn't mean she listened, she just watched, haughtily enduring.

So it was with unusual, clear shock that Kayla called Tyler at his office.

Tyler snatched up the phone and demanded, "Kayla! Are you all right?"

"Of course."

"Kayla—"

"Hush!" And she told him, "Roses were a mistake. Goldilocks is not a wimpy woman. You need something stronger."

"She didn't like the roses?"

"She put them in the trash."

"Wow. She's mad at me!"

And irritated, Kayla explained him to himself, "You didn't *tell* her anything. You evaded and slid aside and were calm, kind and organized. While you're a superior lawyer, you're not a communicator."

"There's a difference?"

Kayla sighed. "Yes."

"Oh."

So he then just hung up the phone. Lawyers are good lawyers but they're not necessarily good person-to-person communicators. However, they can solve just about any problem.

Next Tyler sent Goldilocks a bouquet of shockingly expensive flowers, semirelated to Black-Eyed Susans. A good, strong, no-nonsense flower.

Goldilocks put them on a round table in the round, tiled, marble, elegant, unused entrance hall...and she ignored them. Rejected them. But the rejection was less than that given the pink roses.

So Tyler went to Martha, the covered-up woman at the law office who tried not to attract men. Tyler told her of his confrontation with an irate woman. And he added, "I need your help. You know lawyers.

I endured a quizzing from the woman and evaded all her vocal lures to bare my soul to her.''

"Barbara?"

"No. Her name's Goldilocks and she rules the Davie household of my wife..."

Stilted, Martha corrected, "Your *ex*-wife."

"Yes," he acknowledged. "I was astounded Goldilocks was offended and left the room when I didn't reply openly to her."

"So."

"So I sent her roses. She trashed them. Then I sent those kind of altered Black-Eyed Susans, and she put them in the entrance hall, which was as far from her kitchen as it could be, and she ignored the flowers. What do I do now?"

Martha didn't even hesitate. She replied, "Tell her how you live and what you do is no one else's business. If she asks you questions that are personal, do not reply. Instead, ask some of her." Then she turned back to her computer.

He was stunned. He said to the back of Martha's head, "You don't know Goldilocks."

Not even turning to him, Martha declared, "She's known to everyone. Keep your position. She'll respect you."

"Are you trying to get me in trouble?"

She turned and looked at him coldly. "Your life is your own. You tell what you want to whom you want to know of you. If you prefer to be your own self, and it is none of anyone's business...don't share anything."

He sat in a strange vacuum. It was true. He didn't need to share himself with anyone but those he wanted to know him. Simple.

He smiled, and he found that Martha had already turned back to her computer, immediately rejecting him! He told the back of her head, "You've been a big help to me. Thank you." And he got up and left her little office.

So he made no further effort at all to soothe Goldilocks.

That apparently made Kayla a little agitated and exceptionally curious. She even phoned Tyler at his office! He was very surprised. "Well, hello, Kayla. What's wrong?" And Tyler saw that Jamie heard the name, turned and listened.

And in Tyler's ear, Kayla said, "You haven't done anything to soothe Goldilocks."

Tyler replied, "I've been busy. Goldilocks doesn't need soothing. She's a nosy woman."

"We love her."

"Why?"

"She takes good care of us."

"She rules."

"While that's true, she sure looks out for us and protects us."

Logically, Tyler supplied, "Like any ruler. All rulers need happy underdogs."

"You shock me."

He advised in a friendly manner, "Rattle your cage."

"I left it."

He chided gently, "That was a marriage. Goldilocks has you all in her power. She's a dictator. You all are the masses. Live your life as you would."

"I am."

And he said softly, "Good luck to you." And he hung up.

Jamie said, "Wow."

Tyler drew a deep breath. "I went to Martha and asked her what to do about Goldilocks. And she told me to do it as I wanted it. I found I didn't want to knuckle down to anybody. I'm a free man."

"I'm impressed."

"This doesn't mean I will rule. This only means that no one will rule me."

"Wow." Jamie repeated.

"I'm ready for Barbara."

"Uhhh, just how do you mean that?"

"I can no longer be intimidated."

Jamie commented thoughtfully, "You're growing up."

And Tyler nodded as he said staunchly, "I'll stand taller. Can I go along with you when you go to the new firm?"

"I'll find out." Jamie grinned. "Welcome to manhood."

"I'll see how it fits."

Jamie said, "You fit already. You only need to understand exactly who you are, in what circumstances, and control it—enough."

And Tyler observed quietly, "Jamie, you're a good man."

Jamie smiled. Their pleased eyes considered each other, and Tyler's smile matched his partner's.

It was a very nice thing for them both.

But Kayla vanished. She did not call him again. And Tyler was unable to contact her at all.

The next assignment on Tyler's agenda was an adoption for a childless couple.

He met Tim and Lisa in a conference room. There, they had no interruptions. The couple had seen the baby, and he was just darling. The Social Service Agency was kind. The parents-to-be were a little older than Tyler.

The pair needed legal advice on their adoption. A good medical report was from the Social Service, but the couple wanted the boy looked over by their own doctor.

Having read the guidelines for such a commitment, Tyler advised them to take the child home and see how it went. They ought to adjust, but slowly.

Tim said, "People who have children aren't necessarily trained for such a thing. They just have the baby."

Tyler said gently to his first experience with an actual adoption, "This baby is a little older and a little more experienced than a newborn."

"How do you know that?" Tim was curious.

Tyler grinned. "I'm an uncle, and anyway, the firm has guidelines I'm to give you. You really should listen and consider. Don't be impulsive."

So the two potential parents talked a while and understood the whole commitment better. Better, actually, than Tyler. He really only knew the legal part of the adoption.

The child had been abandoned in a mall. There was no background on the unknown parents. When found, he was such a new little child that the county doctor could say exactly how old he was.

There was no birth certificate. It had not been a medically supervised birth. There was no clue as to parents or if there were siblings. The newspapers had carried pictures of the baby and how he'd been found.

But they only said at a mall. Those who came to claim him could not say the location or describe the birthmark.

There was no birthmark.

The Social Service had placed the baby with a family for care. The family was one who harbored children until they could be adopted.

The potential mother Lisa said, "He's so precious that I wonder how the mother could have given him up...and why. The doctor said he's in good shape."

Tim added, "His coordination is good. He's got a great smile. He listens."

Lisa considered, "It would probably be better if we adopted two at the same time. One could be lonely after being with other kids the way he's been."

Tyler asked, "Could you handle two?"

Tom laughed. "We're wobbled over having one!"

So as they'd parted and Tyler had all the information he needed, he told the two he would be available for any questioning and not to hesitate to call him. They shook hands. And Tyler found he was a bit envious of them. He thoughtfully returned to his office.

Jamie didn't look up from his computer. He just asked, "How'd it go?"

Tyler thoughtfully told Jamie, "They're nice kids."

"Younger than you?"

"Older."

"Then they'll probably be good parents."

In some defense, Tyler said levelly, "I'm old enough to be a good parent!"

Jamie still hadn't looked up from his computer's

screen. He said readily, "I didn't say otherwise. Only they've thought about kids and have come to this conclusion. I admire them for it."

"Me, too." And Tyler set about the papers. But he was curious enough that he made time, a day or so later, to go and see the baby. Tyler didn't hold the baby. He didn't poke his stomach with a teasing finger or tickle his cheek. But Tyler looked at the baby. The little boy was sound asleep, and Tyler smiled.

He asked the woman caring for the kid, "Is he okay?"

She nodded in agreement of that and added verbally, "A nice, sparkling-eyed kid. His body functions are excellent. He breathes well. He moves everything. He is so curious. I've warned them of that. He'll need to know *why* all the way along!"

It was Tyler's first adoption and it felt nice to be a part of something good. Something permanent that would grow and have interesting ramifications.

Of course, that could be said of the businesses that were 'born' and grew. But this was a new little human child.

That made Tyler thoughtful. The adoptive boy had all the needed parts. He was curious. He'd have good parents. And Tyler was satisfied. The new little person was a lucky kid.

So Tyler spent some time phoning around for Kayla, and he finally contacted her. He said thoughtfully, "Maybe we ought to have a kid."

Kayla was startled. "We're divorced!"

"Lots of people who aren't married have kids."

"And you'd come over occasionally and say to the kid whose name you're not positive ab—"

"I'd know his name."

She echoed the gender thoughtfully, "His."

"Her?"

"What would you care which it was?"

"Well, we ought to start off with a boy. He'd take care of his sister."

She was somewhat too emphatic. She told him in a straight, clear manner, "We're divorced. Children should have two parents."

"I'd be around enough."

Kayla scoffed, "Mostly gone."

"Now, Kayla, *most* men work. You wouldn't want me to quit working and hang around the house." Then he paused before he inquired, "If neither of us worked, would your inheritance cover all that?"

"I don't use it—I invest it."

And he congratulated her, "Good thinking. When the kids grow up, we'll be able to get them through college."

Again she mentioned, "We are divorced."

"You're an old-fashioned girl."

She denied that. "I'm a current woman, and I am single. There is no way, at all, that I'd take on having a kid in this position."

He sighed into the phone. "So. I suppose we ought to be married."

"No, thank you. I've tried that." And she hung up.

Women are so strange. Their thinking was a-way off base. What man could figure a woman? She'd left him because he'd taken an interest in stretching her understanding of other people. She was a limited woman. If he was smart, he'd look around for someone else.

He thought with the good advice the self-shielded

Martha had given him, that she would be open to him. Martha was not. She replied through her teeth very negatively and walked off, leaving Tyler standing alone in the office hall. Although there were people walking in different directions and busy, Tyler was then alone in the hall.

Women didn't do that. They didn't just go off and desert a man that way. They were supposed to move slightly to display themselves. So they glanced around, giving a man time to notice them and look down their bodies without the women knowing the guys were looking that way. Martha sure as hell wasn't interested, but why couldn't Kayla be the way a woman should be? Women were baffling.

In San Antonio, the baseball season was almost all year long because the TEXAS weather is so great. The players didn't have to go south for spring training. They were already there. Well, there was a short hiatus in the Christmas season. Otherwise, they played ball.

It was good exercise. The families went and cheered and visited and ate all sorts of expensive trash. Tyler's grandparents exclaimed over the accelerated current cost of hot dogs and beer.

Anyone would think they'd bring their own snacks. They didn't. They paid for the expensive hot dogs and beer, and then they groused. It gave them something to comment about. And along with the rest of his kin and friends, they cheered for Tyler.

He continued batting well enough to bring in others, and on occasion he stole bases or was advanced by the other batters around the bases for a run, but he still did not have a home run. He tried. He swung hard, but the ball wasn't eager enough to go far enough out of reach.

Besides his grandparents, his parents and siblings relentlessly attended. Cousins. Aunts and uncles. Friends. The pack helped fill the bleachers. The overflow people brought folding chairs. They booed and groused at the players and cheered, but they mostly herded their kids or separated them and visited among themselves.

Tyler didn't pay much attention to the crowd after he knew Kayla wasn't there. He muttered to himself that, with their divorce, she'd shunned watching him play ball. Her absence was probably why he couldn't hit a home run.

Well, hell, he hadn't hit one when she was there. Why did he expect to get a homer when she wasn't there?

He'd probably finally swat a home run when she wasn't watching, and she'd never realize that he could hit one. She would never know. That was too bad.

When he finally hit one, maybe he could talk the newspaper into commenting on the home run. The whole story with a picture of him swinging the bat. Yes.

However, the sports editors and reporters were never around for long. They came late and took notes.

If Tyler ever got in the paper with a home run, he'd want to pose for a picture. He could swing the bat. It would look like he'd just hit the ball.

From his office, the next day, Tyler called the newspaper but he had a hard time tracking down the reporter, Omar. When Tyler finally accomplished that little fact, he asked the reporter, "You going out to the games at the parks this year?"

"Maybe."

"Why don't you come on out? Bring your family. I'll treat you to a beer."

Omar stated it with disgust: "You want your pitchur in the paper." He actually called it that.

"I'm divorced."

Omar inquired, softly snide, "You trying to lure somebody?"

"My parents would love a picture of me in the paper."

"Yeah, but it's you that wants the pitchur."

Tyler lost his aloof manner. "Hey! You'd give me a copy of the blowup?"

"For a decent price."

"How much?" Tyler was cautious.

"I'll see."

Thoughtfully, Tyler commented, "I don't think it ought to be life-size."

Omar laughed as he hung up.

Once a week, after work, Tyler would go out to play baseball. He was alert and diligent as a player. However, being on second base, he could glance along the sidelines and out on the field and he'd note any movement in the stands.

He understood he was watching for Kayla to come watch him. Why would she do that? Would she? Nah. He ought to give it up.

There was no indication, at *all*, that she still had any interest in him. He'd filed the divorce to get her attention, but she hadn't even seemed to notice. And now, she was distanced from him. She had put herself out of his reach.

It was sad.

* * *

Tyler began to seriously look around at other women. He went places in a protective group of his longtime friends. Watching the women, he noticed who spoke and who was aloof. Women didn't cotton to divorced men too well. If the man was divorced, there was something wrong somewhere, and women blamed it on the man.

Why would they do that? A guy worked his butt off to feed and clothe a woman, and she divorced him the first chance she had.

Kayla hadn't asked for any alimony. But Kayla had her own money. She didn't need him. She was newly unhitched from him, and now she was free and clear of any husband. She could do whatever she wanted. He had no control over her.

He'd *never* had any control over her, at *all!*

What—all—was she doing?

He and his buddies from grade school went everywhere she might be and looked for Kayla. While Tyler slouched along with his hands in his pockets, he would grind his teeth and be shocked because he never found her.

When he called for her, Henrietta said her roomie was busy with work and not dating much at all.

Hennie would lie. She was a cat-loving, compassionate woman and she'd lie so a rejected ex could feel good.

Of course, it was Tyler who had divorced Kayla. He needed to remember that. It had been his idea as a way to catch her attention. Dumb. He still had to grow up a little.

He couldn't wait to change himself. If he waited

very long, she'd be married next to some useless,
money-sucking guy.

But to "casually run across her" was a problem.
Tyler even slid his way—solo—into a Davie gathering, in hopes of finding Kayla. She wasn't there.

So he called her. Only Hennie answered their
phone. She never knew where Kayla was at that time.
She said *every* time, "I'll tell her you called."

But Kayla never called back.

Tyler *had* divorced *her.*

Well, he'd wanted her attention. With the threat of
divorce, she ought to have come to him on her knees.

No one had ever seemed to understand his divorce
move was to garner her attention. They all just
thought he was stupid. His dad had been disgusted
with him.

And while his mother knew he was far beyond
Kayla, she also thought he wasn't working with a full
deck and took after his daddy's side of the family.

"You're very like your father's cousin Douthit,"
his mother had warned. "He's never shown any real
understanding of *any*thing. It would be very like *him*
to divorce such a woman. Although, unlike you,
Douthit has never been that stupid. He has clung to
Sylvia through everything. I don't know how many
times she's filed for divorce, and he's talked her out
of it. Perhaps you should seek him and discuss your
problem with…Douthit?"

"Mother," Tyler had said earnestly. "I am your
child."

And his mother had observed him stonily and finally replied, "Yes. I know."

A nothing reply that was hardly a vote of approval.

Tyler's brothers and sisters found him stupid. They

scoffed and snorted and didn't even listen to his side
of it. Kayla *had* left him. She and the four dogs she'd
bought at the pit. She'd driven away with the dogs in
his car, leaving him there. And in the morning, she
had been gone. She and the four briefly acquired
dogs.

Besides his brothers, the only staunch, noncritical
acquaintances Tyler had were the dregs of his child-
hood friends. A couple of them were divorced. None
of them offered Tyler any advice or criticism. They
were simply around.

And on occasion, his brothers were along. It was
the same way. His brothers were there. They talked
to his friends and to him about everything, but none
ever mentioned Kayla.

Members of his male support group went along
with whatever Tyler wanted. They were tolerant.
They didn't roll their eyes or sigh, they just went
along and were around. He had good brothers and
good friends.

His sisters were a lot like his parents. Females are
strange. If a man could just reprogram their thought
processes— But even his kindergarten buddies
doubted that would work. And his brothers just
laughed over such a plan in a kind, gentle way.

By purest accident, Tyler asked a cousin of hers,
"Where's Kayla?"

And her cousin replied, "Oh, she's gone ballooning with Tom Keeper, I believe, out west of here."

"She's *what?*" Tyler didn't know which was
worse, her being in a hot-air balloon or being with
Tom Keeper. *Finders keepers, losers weepers!* Where
had that thought come from? Was his subconscious
telling him he was the odd man out?

Six

So the next morning, Tyler went downtown. He drove into the tiered parking garage and eased the nose of his car into his allotted slot on the slightly fanned corner. The time would come when he had the clout to assume he'd be given one of the wider, parallel slots.

Without even having to consider his route, Tyler went through the car maze, down the elevator, out of the garage, down the street, into the firm's building and up to his shared office.

If he'd had to think about doing all that, he probably would have gotten lost. It was his giving in to his directional brain that got him where he was to go. His brain was mapped. And if he didn't interfere with it, he got where he was supposed to go.

Along the way, he had nodded to greetings without

ever knowing he did that. And he responded in a rote manner to Jamie's automatic "Good morning."

But Tyler's distracted reply caused Jamie to look up from his usual concentration as to what was on his desktop. He frowned at Tyler. "What's going on?"

Not even lifting his eyes, Tyler said through his teeth, "She's gone ballooning with that damned bastard."

Jamie knew who the "she" probably was so he just inquired, "Who's...the damned bastard?"

Tyler muttered through his teeth in a very hot-tempered way, "Tom Keeper."

"I hadn't known he was a bastard." In his mild exclamation, Jamie was being subtly chiding. "If fact, I met his parents not—"

Distracted, ordering his papers, Tyler growled, "For Keeper, being a bastard isn't necessarily genetic."

Watching Tyler's hunt, Jamie inquired carefully, "What paper are you looking for?"

And Tyler still didn't look up. "I'm separating my workload so Miss Nelson can spread it out. You'll probably get the most of it."

"I'll help her. Give the files to me."

"Thank you." Tyler put the stack down on Jamie's desk. He finally looked at Jamie.

And Jamie, oddly enough, was not looking at his papers as he generally did. He was looking right at Tyler. And he was very serious.

Tyler told Jamie, "I'm going out to where they're ballooning."

"You're going to have to ask Barb for time. And she'll ask why and where you'll be."

"She's damned nosy."

"Careful." Jamie's voice was very soft. "Anyone who is in charge must know where the crew is. She'll need to know where you'll be, for how long and she will ask why."

"Family business."

Jamie considered. "She may not accept only that."

"I'll quit."

"The firm we're going to isn't yet ready for us."

The kind manner of Jamie's reply caused Tyler's eyes to focus on his partner. "Yes." Tyler took a steadying breath. "I'm a little rattled. I wasn't being logical. Thank you."

"You're welcome. Tell me what you plan to do. Are you carrying a gun?"

"No. For Pete's sake, Jamie. I'm not—I wouldn't use a gun. I might throttle the guy, but I wouldn't shoot him."

Stoically, Jamie commented, "That problem is out of the way." But he continued his intense concentration on Tyler. "Now tell me what you *plan* to do. First, tell me where they are ballooning at this time of the year."

Tyler replied readily but with an inpatient movement of one hand, "Out west."

"Out...west." Jamie's hesitated, underlined echo was deliberate. "That covers quite a bit of territory. West TEXAS is rather large. You need to be more specific."

"I'll call in."

The reply was okay, but Jamie knew it was vague and probably Tyler would not remember to call in. So Jamie inquired bluntly, "What route do you take?"

And being a TEXAN, Tyler parroted quickly, "I-10."

Hell, that old trail was a longtime track that had been turned into a highway. It went from Florida to California. Anybody knew that. Jamie was more specific. "—and you turn off...where?"

Tyler looked up with such innocent eyes that Jamie could have kicked him. Tyler said logically, "It'll be along the highway."

"You'll just go tooling along those hundreds of miles and stop when you see the balloons?"

Tyler's stoney eyes considered his pushy office mate. Tyler said a hostile, "Yeah." It sounded like a matchstick on his shoulder.

"You don't know where the ballooning starts or which way the wind is blowing."

"I'll find out."

"Let's do that now."

"Jamie." It was a serious warning.

However, Jamie ignored that and just picked up his phone. He punched in a number he knew. It was the weather station at the airport. He asked, "Can you tell me if there are any balloon races out west of here?" He listened and wrote on a page. He said, "I see." He listened some more. "Ummm." He was silent again. "Yeah." And he said, "Thank you."

As Jamie hung up, he looked at Tyler. "What's the name of her ballooning group?"

"Huh?"

Looking at the paper on which he'd jotted notes, he asked more specifically, "Which group is she with?"

And Tyler's gaunt face was a total blank. He was

sunk. He lowered his eyes to his desk and just stood there.

Jamie got up but he did not come closer. He said, "There are five different, organized groups slated for today. These are out from the other side of Uvalde and on beyond. It must be a good day...but then all days in TEXAS are good days."

Tyler did not respond to that old saw at all.

Jamie said, "You could call Tom's office and see which race he's in."

Tyler's sad eyes rose to look at Jamie. "I'd have to give my name."

"I'll call."

"Tom's people know you."

"You want to sneak in? Tyler, you have to know a balloon race is not in one place. They *are* balloons. They lift off and float to various places."

Tyler looked down at his desk. He had nothing to say. He was zonked.

Jamie said, "Let's go out for coffee."

"She'll kill us."

"Barbara?" Jamie grinned. "If her guards notice we're gone, it'll be an excuse to be in her office and having her talk at me." His smile widened. "When I leave here, I'm going to womannap her for lunch."

In some intense curiosity, Tyler asked, "You're going to *eat* her?"

Jamie laughed. "I'm going to have a farewell meal with her. She can't refuse. It would be rude of her and she has good manners."

That last sentence made Tyler blink. He didn't know of a more rude and outspoken woman in all his life! It showed his regard for Jamie in that Tyler didn't make any comment. He bit his lower lip to keep from saying anything at all. It wasn't entirely courteous self-control. It was because Jamie watched him with a deadly eye.

Jamie's conduct and concern for Tyler was an indication that Jamie wouldn't reject his friendship with Tyler any more than he'd reject his love for that woman. Love was something no human person could guide or control. What was...*was!*

Even Tyler was guilty of such a lack of logic and control. He loved that awful, snotty, independent woman Kayla.

Ummmm. That was two women Tyler didn't see as being fine, gentle women. Could this rejective attitude be...from him? Was he the culprit of critical hostility?

Naw.

He was a decent, levelheaded, well-bred man. He'd been taught what was proper and what was not.

His dad tended to be profemale, especially with Kayla. He called her the darlin' and missed having her around.

Tyler had been raised like the gentle man that he was. He protected women and country. Actually, the country came first. If you didn't have a country, a man might not have a woman. So establishing and protecting the country was vital.

Along with the country, and women, he was for justice and men's rights. Uhhh. Women's rights also, but he needed to monitor the list.

And just because he'd gone through with the threatened divorce, Kayla hadn't lifted one finger to beg his forgiveness.

Women are underhanded and strange. No man should be tied to a woman. He ought to see one now and then to give her children. He did have to be sure the kids were being raised properly. And see the woman just to realize the female conduct wasn't only his imagination.

So in his thinking, he rose to stand erect as Barbara Nelson came into the office to speak to him. She ignored the standing Jamie. What a witch.

Tyler looked dismissively at Miss Nelson, and she smiled. He said in a level voice, "My eardrums are burst. I cannot hear anything." He said that through her own speech—which he could hear perfectly well.

He was so disgusted with everything—not getting to leave and search for Kayla and now having such a woman come into the office—that he was really ticked. He thought of the deafness excuse without any problem at all. He said, "Tell it to Jamie." And he went out of the room. Just like that.

Jamie found Tyler in the parking garage, getting into his car. Jamie got in on the other side of the backing car. He took the keys out of the ignition. That stalled the car, right there, half in and half out of Tyler's slot.

Jamie said, "What the *hell* are you doing?"

"*You* took the keys."

"I had to stop you. Where are you going?"

And Tyler explained quite kindly. "I believe I'm going into rebellion. I didn't at twelve or at fourteen or even at sixteen like most males. And I have never declined my duty. I am now in revolt."

Jamie said with equal gentleness, "You're not in revolt, you're acting like a jackass. Cut it out and come back to the office. We got the Anderson trial."

Tyler looked at Jamie with naked eyes. He asked softly, "The *Anderson* trial?"

"Yep."

Tyler got out the driver's side as he said, "I get the final argument!"

"Like hell! Come back here and put the car back in your slot."

Tyler walked off, saying, "You've got the keys, *you* do it!"

Nothing more was said. Tyler walked on off down to the elevator. Jamie got out of the car and went around to get into the driver's seat...and he adjusted the seat just so. Then he put the car back where it belonged. But he didn't readjust anything.

At their office, Jamie said, "You forgot your keys."

Tyler replied, "I was a bastard. This is a puberty throwback. I won't ask your forgiveness. I'll do something brilliant and say it was you who did it."

"I'll do my own work. Take care of yourself. If you're over this particular hump, I will survive. If you go into another, I'll break your damned neck."

Tyler laughed.

Jamie sat down and watched the laugh, and his own eyes crinkled. He said, "Behave. We have a hell of a schedule on this one."

Tyler agreed with a nod but he said, "It'll be shared. I'm proud to be a part of it with you."

"Are you trying to smooth things out?"

"No. I'm being honest."

"Me, too."

They shook hands silently. They both were sparkling-eyed and excited. This would be their trial of the century. Tyler asked, "Can we win?"

And Jamie replied, "Of course. And we should. I believe in them and their situation."

"Wow. That's the way a lawyer should be with a client. I remember when our law prof said—"

"Hush." Jamie sat down and began on his papers. He added to Tyler, "We need to clear this off as much as possible, and get to the Anderson case as soon as we get the first box. And then we need to meet the family and listen. We need to have the list of questions and what they've said to the other lawyers in the firm."

"How did we get—this—case?"

"Barbara."

"So she finally recognizes what a good, diligent lawyer... *you* are." Tyler grinned. "Fooled you there, didn't I?"

Never looking up, moving the papers on the top of his desk and organizing them carefully, Jamie said, "No, you didn't fool me. I agree. I am a good lawyer. You're going to be. You still have some rough edges and you need to mature."

"Oh, hell."

Jamie returned the papers Tyler had given him. Still busy, his voice slowing, Jamie said softly, "It's true. I'll guide you along."

Tyler shook his head. He began to reorganize his desk. He could do that and think also of what a strange day it had been. He'd planned to skip the office and go find Kayla, out riding some hot-air balloon with a bastard named Keeper, and here he was, half of a team for a big trial.

He asked Jamie, "What's the trial date?"

"We have four months, and the trial is scheduled for two weeks...maybe three."

Tyler commented, "Sounds serious."

"What trial isn't?"

Tyler mused, "I've never done any longer than a couple of days."

"This will be so intense, you'll forget the time."

And Tyler said, "I've got to play baseball once a week. If I don't, I go into a decline."

So Jamie promised, "You'll get to play. We can't have a good lawyer in a decline."

Then Tyler looked at Jamie in such a way that Jamie glanced over at him. He asked Tyler, "You okay, now?"

"I was just thinking how this day started and what all you've done for me in this time. Thank you, Jamie."

Jamie grinned. "High five." The celebrating meeting of hands held high.

So they were immersed in the Anderson trial. It was intense. Their time was hard used. But Jamie saw to it that Tyler played ball every Thursday. Therefore, since he could play only on Thursday, the rest of the team had to adjust to Tyler. They switched with another team that cheerfully groused about it. Nobody on his team complained or bellyached. That warmed the cockles of Tyler's heart.

Some of the team said, "How's it going?" Or they said, "Kin to William Jennings Bryan or Clarence Darrow?" And Tyler replied gently, "Not exactly blood kin."

So in that time, Tyler did play ball. In that first month, he was out on second base and who should come into the stands but *Kayla!* Not that she rattled him. He would have probably missed that fly ball anyway.

But *then* Tyler saw that she was with *Tom Keeper!* What was she doing running around the countryside with that wealthy trash? Tyler was so shocked that he wouldn't look at them again. He didn't for one minute want Tom to think *he* was jealous. He—was—not!

Tyler did not look at them even once. He didn't hear what was being said because he was sure the other guys were talking about Kayla being with Tom, and Tyler didn't know what to do about something like that. How could he hit a teammate?

When it was Tyler's turn at bat, he was so furious that he hit a home run with two men on base!

He grimly went around the bases as the standing crowd roared and screamed and carried on like they'd never seen a home run before then! Well, they hadn't...from him.

And the whole entire team was lined up at home plate to shake his hand and swat him on the back. They really overdid it. They laughed and hugged him and really acted silly.

Because the coach insisted, Tyler rose from the bench that was their "dugout" and stepped out to raise his hat to the cheering crowd. And he sneaked one look at where Kayla was...with Tom Keeper.

She was not there. When had they left? Tyler took a longer bow to the cheerfully cheering people. Kayla was nowhere around.

And Tyler was even more silent after that. All of his team knew he was on the Anderson trial, and they attributed Tyler's sobriety to that trial.

The disappointment was that Kayla hadn't seen his home run—with two batted in. And he admitted to himself that the home run had been for Kayla. To show off for her over that damned Keeper. What was she doing with Keeper? What *all* was she doing with him? With that hungry body of hers. With another man. How could she?

His picture was in the paper. *Every*body knew he'd hit a home run—if she read the paper.

In the following weeks, Tyler became the Home Run Kid. He hit five home runs in that time. Everyone on his team was exuberant. They got runoff fever. When the final games came, with Tyler hitting that way, they'd win the county championship!

Tyler didn't give a damn. He just swung at the ball, and it went off on its own in a beautiful arc that went over the fence and evaded any fielder.

The miracle became irritating to Tyler. He really didn't care about the hitting, that much. He'd survived the games with a good plus. Now the jubilant team treated him like a prince. The team and the coaches were exuberant. They loved him.

And he was glum. He was silent. At work, he did his share and better. He was concentrated and a good lawyer. He paid attention to every detail. He was careful and made the research into all questions and found the answers. His diligence was like a fine-tooth comb.

Not even bothering to look at him, Jamie told Tyler, "Barbara is impressed with our work. She reads what we've done every day. She thinks we are better than the top brass. She says she's never seen a brief so perfectly done. She calls me Jamie. She knows my name."

In a dead voice, Tyler said, "Hallelujah."

Jamie turned his chair around and looked at Tyler. "When I told you to settle down, I didn't think you'd go sour. You must be suffering to be this sour. Is it Kayla?''

And Tyler was honest. "Yeah."

So Jamie told Tyler, "Send her an invitation for dinner. Have flowers and order the dinner made and delivered just right. She'll melt." And finished, Jamie turned back to his desk.

"You do that with Miss Nelson?"

Not bothering to look up from the papers on his desk, Jamie admitted briefly, "We've had dinner at my place."

"Ahhhh."

Jamie warned, "Hush. Any talk and you could spoil everything."

So Tyler volunteered, "I'll quit calling her Miss Nelson and call her Barb."

Still concentrated on the papers, Jamie shook his head. "No. You continue being distant."

Tyler nodded and said, "Right."

"See to it until I have time to seal her up."

That alerted Tyler. "Aren't we moving to the other firm?"

"Maybe not." Jamie looked up.

"Oh, hell." But Tyler grinned at Jamie, who looked smug.

Then Tyler asked, "With our agenda so pressed and serious, how do you have time to court Miss Nelson?"

But Jamie was back to the papers before him. He said, "Be quiet."

"I just wondered about—"

"You play baseball, right?"

Tyler squinted his eyes. "I don't see any similarity between baseball and—"

"Never mind."

Tyler complained, "Man, you're touchy!"

"Hush."

And Tyler really laughed for the first time in...how long had it been?

So Tyler called Kayla at work and for once, she answered the phone. Tyler said quickly, "Don't hang up!"

"Hello, Tyler."

And he asked softly, "How'd you know?"

"No one else expects me to hang up on him."

So he asked, "You get a lot of male calls?"

"Why did you call?"

He had to change lanes mentally, but he said, "Come for dinner on Saturday."

"I have an appointment."

Tyler gasped, "Appointment? *Appointment!* Who the hell're you dating?"

Patiently, Kayla explained, "I'm being interviewed for another job."

"On Saturday?" His tone was unbelieving. And he inquired in a rather snotty way, "Just what sort of interview does he have in mind?"

"She is traveling and is coming by to check me out."

His voice changed markedly. "She?"

"Yes."

So then, being male, he asked, "Who's she work for?"

"It's her business."

He felt that was a closed door. "Well, I just asked—"

Kayla said patiently, "She owns the business."

"Oh." There was a silence. But Kayla didn't hang

up. She was waiting. So Tyler asked, "Could you come to dinner the next Saturday?"

Instead of replying to that, she mentioned, "I hear you're on the Anderson case."

"Yeah."

And she said, "I am impressed. Did that witch Barbara lure you with the trial?"

With some chiding, Tyler replied, "She's dating Jamie."

"Does Jamie's family know about Barbara the witch?"

"Uhhhh." Tyler sought the acceptable words, "We may have to adjust to Jamie's love for her."

"No! Jamie? A good man drawn into that witch's net? Can't you help him?"

Bored by then, Tyler replied, "I wouldn't even try."

"You're not at all loyal. I can vouch—"

Very gently, he assured Kayla, "Jamie loves her. He won't even allow me to say one word in opposition to the wi—lady."

"Wow!"

"It boggles me," Tyler mentioned.

"I can understand it. I've got you down for a week from Saturday. What time?"

"Two—a.m.?"

She laughed.

So he inquired, "After all this time, do you still like ribs and slaw?"

"No. I'm for steak, French fries and a salad."

He sounded distracted as if he was writing it down. He said, "Got it."

"What time?"

He replied easily, "I'll pick you up at Hennie's about...five-thirty?"

"No, I'll drive. Early supper?"

His voice was foggy. "We'll have a lot to talk about. I'm glad I'll see you again. Take care."

"You, too. Thank you for inviting me. I'll look forward to it."

But he couldn't so easily let her go. He told her, "As I remember, you like your meat well done."

And Kayla replied, "Yes."

He put the menu on his voice box to record what was needed.

At their apartment, uh, *his* apartment, he was surprised the place turned up so much dirt and dust and newspapers. He blinked and wondered at that. And he asked the apartment manager, "What's with the apartment cleaners?"

And the manager looked up and asked back, "What apartment cleaners?"

That stopped Tyler for a minute. "You mean nobody's been cleaning my apartment?"

The manager replied, "Not this year."

And Tyler said, "Oh."

"Remember the thievery? You all had a meeting and decided we'd just do our own? You organized the meet."

"I did?"

"It was just after she left you. What's her name again?"

"Mrs. Fuller."

"No. What'd she go back to?"

And Tyler declined to say, so he just repeated, "Mrs. Fuller."

"Uh. Yeah." Then the manager cautioned, "You need some help in facing the little fact that you divorced her and she's gone."

Tyler didn't reply but gently left the office. So that was why the place wasn't very tidy. Well, he could clean an hour at a time and get it done. He closed his eyes and remembered being a scout. He could do it. And he remembered his mother's narrowed eyes as she told him to get his room cleaned up right *then!* She told him through her teeth that he could not leave the house until it was done. And then his daddy said very similar things but in a different way.

Hmmmm.

So when he finally got home, and it was always late, he looked at his apartment. And he realized he hadn't been paying much attention. The loaded dining-room table should have been a clue. He began.

Tyler worked until the time-beep sounded. It was time for him to go to bed. He felt a little like the automated ancient film of Charlie Chaplin, his coping with the humongous machine and the whistle that marked the end of the working day.

There was no difference. Only the whistle was now a beep. Of course, Tyler wasn't coping with a machine at the office, he was coping with filing. At home, it was with discarding…with carelessness. It became a challenge.

His only problem was that at the office, he got caught up in reading things he was filing.

He needed better self-discipline.

He *had* discipline. Now. Not the last time he had Kayla there in his apartment, he had loved his partially disrobed ex-wife. He looked out of the room's door to the living room and on beyond the living room to the cars passing on the street.

How had his life come to this?

What had been the first clue that his marriage was crumbling? What would he have done if he'd noted it?

He'd never dreamed there would be this split. These problems. He'd thought he and Kayla were perfect for each other and that she'd loved him.

How could she have left him so finally? Well, he *had* divorced her.

Why had she now agreed to come to dinner with him?

And he figured it out. She'd decided she wanted alimony after all.

Seven

For Tyler, the cleaning of his apartment was exhilarating. The high was rather remarkable to anyone who has the time for it and has cleaned up his room or place. Most apartments aren't that big. With the intruding junk in smaller habitats, there is no choice. It has to be discarded, and it can be.

The accumulations of potentially fascinating things that could be thrown away was something Tyler had never considered. When he'd lived at home, and was given no alternative but to clean his room, his mother had pitched what he had set aside as not vital. So the actual act of discarding something hadn't been ingrained in Tyler's thinking. That was probably why his desk at work was such a mess.

He decided that when he finished with the Anderson trial, he'd attack his filing cabinets and his desk. His desk would have to be first. The desktop. With the top cleaned off, he could then empty the drawers. And, he supposed, after that would be the renovation of his file cabinets.

Tyler remembered reading some bright illusion of proliferating papers which doubled each night in the silent dark. That was more than likely true. He'd seen that it had happened in just such a way on his own desk.

He wondered if he was maturing.

Maturity had been a milestone until he was about twenty-five, several years ago. Now he felt longer in the tooth. He'd become a thoughtful, understanding human being. Yes.

Kayla was younger than he. He could help her over this blockage of youth and lead her into adulthood. It would be soothing to know a woman who had pushed away from adolescence to float free.

The intense concentration of preparing for the Anderson trial was without comparison for Tyler. Jamie was riveted but loose enough. Tyler's plotted distraction was clearing out his apartment. It refreshed his thinking—enough—and he felt the lift of orderliness, of accomplishment. Of something else that was different from the rules of law.

Of course, tidiness was another rule. And he considered all the rules by which we live. Traffic, food, dress, conduct and all the others of honesty, compassion, and even distaste of wrongs.

Rules.

Those of law. Those rules of others. The clash which countering laws invoked. War.

Life was never simple.

And Kayla should come back under his supervision so that she could mature more easily.

What the *hell* was she doing out ballooning with *Keeper!*

She needed to reject Keeper and come back to him.

So it was on Saturday of that next week, when Kayla drove to his place. She was astonished by the changes in the apartment. She even checked the number on the apartment door. She asked, "Who did you find to clean up this place? I need to know the crew."

And he stopped and turned his head to say with surprise, "Does it look different to you?"

"It's neat and clean."

And Tyler looked around as if to check it out. He frowned a little. Then he had the audacity to ask, "What's different?"

"Who did you find to clean it this well? How did they manage to get rid of all the stuff on the dining-room table?" She touched her hand to the already set table. No tablecloth, just place mats, and a humongous bouquet of gladiolas.

"Oh." He looked thoughtful. "I did that while I was sorting things out on the table. It didn't take long."

"It must have taken a *week!*"

He shook his head thoughtfully. "Naw. It was nothing. We'll eat in here."

"With the table set so beautifully, I figured we'd probably eat here." Then with no snorts, she said of the great sweep of gladiolas, "The flowers are lovely. Shall I put them to one side so that we can see each other?"

His regard of the flowers was supposed to be serious, but his smile began. His dancing eyes looked at her, and they both laughed.

She moved the flowers to one side of the table. The bouquet was still intrusive, but with moving them over, the two people would be able to see each other without stretching up and straining their necks.

Kayla was so amused.

Their conversation widened and they spoke of people they knew. They replied to questions of friends who one or the other hadn't seen, and they talked about siblings.

The meal was eaten but neither of them would have been able to comment on the food other than to admit it was gone. Since there would be no complaint, the meal had to have been okay.

Of course, Tyler could cook steaks exactly right. No one can ruin baked yams, and the salad was perfect. A little ragged and some of the pieces required cutting, but the rolls were excellent and so was everything else.

Kayla inquired, "Your mother's rolls? They surely taste that perfect."

"She loves you, too."

Kayla smiled. She saw his parents every week.

Kayla told him all the gossip about their shared friends, and he was *shocked!*

Kayla asked, "Now, how could you be surprised? They've been together how long now, a year and a half? Two years?"

"But I didn't think they were *serious!*"

Kayla waved a hand in the air as if to discourage a bee. "You sound just like a gossip."

He was sure. "Men never gossip."

She snorted. "They spread the word, the specula-
tion—"

"Men only tell the facts."

Her laugh was softly controlled, with true humor.
Her eyes danced and she tried not to burst with the
hilarity.

And he knew what else he missed in not seeing
her. He became serious, watching her. Her attraction
was so potent. Godzilla agreed. Tyler breathed carefully so that he wouldn't frighten her with urgent,
basic, hungry sounds.

His hunger was not for food.

In the strange silence, with her like a bird unaware
of the cleverly moving, freezing still and stalking cat
that he was, she chewed the carefully cooked steak
and then blotted her lips. She said, "You really know
steaks. This one is perfect."

"You're welcome."

She lifted her eyebrows a little as she looked down.
"Any woman cook would know to disclaim perfec-
tion."

"I'm an honest man."

She almost smiled. "You're a jealous, stubborn
man."

And he agreed, "That, too."

So she asked seriously, "Why on earth would you
be jealous of me?"

"Not of you, but of the man with you."

She looked around the room. "No one else is
here."

"I hit a home run because of you."

"I saw it. I cried. Tom took me away so I wouldn't
seem so foolish. You're a brilliant batter."

He gasped. "You *saw* it?"

"Of course! And I've watched the other home runs."

His eyes were vulnerable. "Where were you?"

"With the family. You've been terrific! I knew you could do it. Did it really take anger before you could hit a home run?"

"I hate Tom Keeper."

"No, you don't. You admire him and like him as a friend.

"No."

"You're acting like a kid in junior high."

"Yeah."

"All testosterone?"

"Overflowing."

She sat back and regarded him seriously. "I know a cure."

"Ice baths?"

She smiled just a little. "No."

How was he to act with that opening? How could he get her into bed with him and vent the bottled-up passionate love that was driving him crazy? And all of a sudden, he came to the conclusion that all he had to do was allow her the freedom of him. He smiled a little, watching her.

She licked her lips and smiled back. She was watching him intently. He prayed, *Don't let the phone ring!*

He asked, "Would it scare you if I stood up?"

"Why...stand up?" Her eyes were sparkling and intent. She was tense and breathing high in her chest. Her breasts were pushy. She was ready.

"I'll stand up...in order to clear the table?"

She gasped. Then she frowned but it was over her

smile. She questioned, ''You want to clear the table—
now?''

''Well, if you don't shock over my standing up, I'll
take it from there.''

''Do it carefully.'' She quickly licked her lips
again.

So, slowly, he did stand up. She looked down his
body and smiled. She licked her already wet lips and
looked back at his face. She said, ''Yeah.''

''Yeah? To what?''

''You.''

His breathing changed to harshness. ''Don't tease
me. Not now.''

''Why not?''

''It would be unkind. I'm really triggered.''

She tilted her head back and observed him. ''There
are ways to solve that.''

''Help me.''

''I believe I'd rather you take control. I feel a little
bashful.''

He didn't laugh. The urge was there, but she'd
turned serious. So he also became serious. Smart men
walked a narrow, careful line.

He went to her and put his hands under her armpits.
He lifted her, with his wrists pushing against the sides
of her pushy breasts. He was quite surprised that he
could do that when she wasn't helping at all.

She was breathing and limp. She was very intense
and serious. She didn't knock his wrists away. She
bowed her back a little as he put her against his chest
and slid her down onto her feet as his mouth followed
hers down and he kissed her.

She breathed and made little sounds. He was
amazed. He'd been sure that she'd be tight and dis-

tanced over having dinner with him. He'd had no idea she would allow him any attentions at all!

The kiss was a rocket. Right through him. Godzilla was about to go off. He said, "Don't tease."

And with closed eyes, she whispered, "Do it."

So he undid her belt with shaky hands and harsh breathing. He unzipped the back of her dress and tugged it off her arms and helped it slide down her satin slip. He said, "You trying to ruin me for any other woman?"

"How could I do that?"

"Just recently, you were in my bed."

"Ummmmm." She said that for whatever it meant.

"You let me."

She wiggled closer.

Holding her tightly against him, he kissed her again. His shirt was off. He didn't remember when he managed that. And his belt was undone and his zipper was opened. She was feeling around in his pants! *She* had done it all! What a body-hungry woman!

His throat made a very pleased sound.

She was gasping. Her eyelids were heavy. She made little moans. He remembered her doing that very thing! She used to do that! It pushed him higher.

He had no trouble lifting her, carrying her. Had she weighed three hundred pounds at that time, he would have lifted her without any thought of it at all. It felt so good to have her in his arms again.

As they entered his room, she saw that the bedroom was pristine. The sheets were crisp and clean. She asked, "Who were you expecting?"

And he said, "Today is sheet day. I send them to the laundry with my shirts."

She looked at him, weighing the truth of him. And he watched her very seriously.

"You didn't plan to seduce me?"

"I hadn't a chance."

"Obviously, you did."

He smiled gently. "I love you."

"Maybe."

She was cooling.

He put her feet on the floor, steadied her and went over to the woven laundry basket. He took off the top of it and tilted it for her to see inside. It bore two hand towels, some underwear and one shirt.

She didn't say anything. She didn't move.

He gave up. He said, "Would you like some ice cream on the pie?" And he looked at her very seriously.

She took her slip at the bottom, lifted it off over her head and discarded it onto the floor. She wore nothing under the slip but a garter belt and stockings.

He remembered her doing that just before they were married. He tilted his head back and groaned.

And she said, "So you haven't lost interest?"

"Have you?"

"You'll have to work a little to get me back in heat."

"Do you think you can sit on a chair and have some hot apple pie okay?"

"You've given up?"

"No. I want you as hot as you were before you decided someone else was going to be here in that bed."

"I've never seen the bed made up when you were here."

"I've changed. I make it every morning. I put the clothes away and I tidy the kitchen."

She tilted her head and looked at him with a slight frown. "How come you've changed?"

"I think it was Jamie. He's a neat man. I decided I should be as neat."

"Had he been here and seen the mess?"

"No."

She frowned. "Then—how did you become—changed?"

"He treats me like an equal. He tells me if I'm wrong, but he doesn't run over me or make me feel inferior."

"You're a superior man."

"Thank you. I believe the time will come when I could be."

She was very thoughtful. "The...time...will come?"

"I've a few more rough edges."

"Do your parents know?"

"They love me. They are tolerant."

"And I was not?"

"I didn't leave you."

And she reminded him soberly, "You divorced me."

"I was trying to get your attention to see how serious your leaving me was to you."

"That's an odd way of doing it."

He agreed. "You're right. I was less mature at that time."

"And now?"

"I've wanted you back from the time you left. That's why I started the divorce. I thought you'd object to it."

Soberly, she told him, "I was stunned."

"Come have some of the apple pie. It's Mother's, so you know it's perfect. I even have some vanilla ice cream."

She commented seriously, "You've given up on getting me into bed?"

"It isn't sex I want. I want you back willingly. Without any doubts about loving me."

"I'm embarrassed."

And his voice was tender. "Don't be. It just wasn't the way we wanted it. Instead of love, it would just be sex. Great, but not the way we wanted it."

Pulling on her slip, she said, "This isn't the first time something has stopped us."

"You really aren't sure of me as yet. The time will come when you are. I'll court you all over again."

She smiled just a sad tad. "All over, again."

"Are you disappointed? Do I make you angry? You shouldn't be. I love you, Kayla. I don't know of a better way of proving it. It isn't sex I want as much as I want you to love me again. Having your body is ecstasy, and it would be so anytime, but I need to know you love me. And even more important than that, you need to know that I really love you."

She frowned a little. "You're becoming mature. I'm not sure I know how to match you."

"You're perfect. You only need to know how much I care for and about you."

Kayla lifted her head back a little. "I believe every woman would thrill at hearing such a declaration, but I'm not sure I'm open to it as yet."

"I hope you will be."

She frowned at Tyler. "You're getting different."

"In what way?"

She shrugged back into her dress as she told him, "I'm not sure." She turned and walked slowly from his room. Their once shared room. But now it was...his.

He sighed and looked down at his anxious sex. He put his hand kindly on Godzilla in sympathy and then pulled on his trousers. He found a shirt which could be worn outside of his trousers, and he stepped into felt slippers.

In his kitchen, Kayla was seriously concentrated in cutting the apple pie. She looked up at Tyler and her face was solemn.

He smiled gently. "I like seeing you here again."

And she replied rather grimly, "You want me to wash the dishes."

He said, "No." He went to her and took the knife from her hand. He thought of his old friend Bill who had always said, "Never give a woman a knife or a gun."

She asked, "Why the smile?"

"I like you being here."

"Doing all the work for you, serving you?"

"You're pushing for a quarrel. Why?"

"I don't know."

"Let's leave the dessert here and go in the living room and talk."

She watched him. "About...what?"

"Oh, life and times and home runs?" He smiled at her so kindly.

Kayla said, "Are you going to seduce me?"

"Not if you don't want to."

"You leave it all up to me? Then you can say that I was the one who started it all."

"I've never known you to be so negative. What's eating you?"

So she told him, "When I let you know I would be with Tom, you didn't come and get me."

"I didn't know where the hell you were, and I was frantic. There were *five* balloon races that day."

"Oh."

And he pushed. "So, you knew I was jealous of Keeper."

"I thought I'd catch your attention."

He nodded in understanding. "I thought you'd protest the divorce. How come you just let me go on and do it? Didn't you want me at all?"

"I wanted you to come after me and demand that I go back with you."

"Like a caveman? I'm a little more advanced than that."

She said, "I dream about you."

He grinned. "Like I dream about you?"

"How do you dream?" She was serious and watched him.

"I dream you come into my room and tear off your clothes as you pull back the sheet and you're all over me."

"Do you protest?"

"I whisper 'help, help.'"

"Not out loud?"

"Somebody might hear me and come to help me get away."

She smiled.

He said, "I can't tell you how nice it is for me to have you here and talking to me."

"You didn't make love to me."

"You'd cooled. When we make love again, I want

you hot and eager, not pulling back and finding fault with me."

"I didn't think you'd care so long as you got what you wanted."

"Ahhh, Kayla, can you be that unknowing? It isn't just sex that I want, it's love. I want you around and well. I want you to visit with me and tell me things. I want you to want me as much and like it. I don't want you to submit. I want you willing and eager."

"You've become…different."

"I believe I'm growing up. It's Jamie who's guided me along. I was on my way to find you and Keeper. Jamie made me find out where you might be…and it's a good thing he did. I had no idea where or which balloon bunch I'd find. There were those five different bunches, that day, along the highway. How would I have ever found you?"

"You could have asked my mother or your mother or just about anyone."

Carefully, he asked, "How did they know?"

"I told them so's you'd know."

"You *wanted* me to find you?"

A little irritated, she said a sharp, "Of course."

And he asked softly, "Why?"

But she replied, "I don't know."

He watched her for a while. Then he told her, "When you find out why, then let me know."

He cut the apple pie and placed it into bowls so that they could put enough ice cream over it.

As they sat at the table and began to eat the ice cream covered pie, she asked, "So your mother knew I'd come to have supper with you?"

"No. She just gave me the pie about six weeks or

so ago. I froze it until I have a good reason to thaw it out.''

"She makes good pies."

He watched Kayla.

She repeated, "She does make good pies."

"I'm waiting for you to tell me that she makes good sons."

"Ego?"

"No. I want to seem special to you."

"Am I special to you?"

"You're the only woman I've ever married."

"What would you do if I chose another man?"

He stilled. Then he looked at her. Finally he asked, "Like Tom Keeper?"

"I hadn't thought about him."

He used his spoon to put more ice cream up onto his pie. He didn't eat. He finally looked up and said, "If you love him, then it would be best if you go with him. I wouldn't want to be second choice."

Her pupils widened in shock. She was very still.

He got up from the table and put the pie in the disposal. He rinsed the plate and put it in the small dishwasher he'd bought over a year ago.

She said, "I only asked a question."

He nodded, standing there seriously with his hands in his pockets. He was solemn and still.

Not able to think of a way to counter the silence, she stood up and picked up the pie. She said, "I'll take the pie home."

He nodded, got a plastic plate and put the pie onto it. He covered it with a paper napkin. As he handed it to her, he said, "I've got some papers to go over for tomorrow."

She said, "Oh."

He went into the living room, and she followed him, carrying the pie. He got her jacket from the pristinely ordered coat closet, and he helped her to put it on. He went to the front door and opened it.

She hesitated. Then she walked out past him and went down the hall to the front door of the building. He got there first and opened it for her, and walked with her across the porch and down the steps. They said a stiff goodbye yet again. He stood at the bottom of the steps and watched her as she went to her car, got in and slowly drove away.

Both of them went into a decline. Kayla was especially so. She did not understand why they were so far apart. After all, he was the one who needed to court her. He'd divorced *her*. He needed to convince her that he loved her.

He had not. He wanted her in bed. But he wouldn't insist. He wanted her eager and willing. Her want matching his. He neglected to sweetly coax her with honeyed words and sweet caresses.

In a blue, discouraged funk, Tyler had gone back to his apartment. He'd changed into jogging clothes and went out to run himself into enough physical exhaustion that he would sleep.

As time had eased past, the structuring of the trial went well. It was simple, clean and true. There was backup for everything. All was researched and proven. It was so well done and clear that it scared Tyler spitless.

What did the opposition have that could counter them? If the opposition knew all the truths, what did they have that could possibly give them the guts to face a trial?

Tyler mentioned that to Jamie. And Jamie went on dealing with papers on his desk as he replied, "They're not paying for the trial, they're being paid."

That was true.

And it finally came time for them to choose the jury.

Trial by jury is a constitutional right. Demand for a jury is a given.

In choosing a jury, there is the challenge for cause and a preemptory challenge. They are different.

In the challenge for cause, the potential juror is questioned. The questions are slid in and if the potential juror gives the wrong answer or sounds like a problem or is prejudiced in the favor of the other side, he or she can be challenged for cause by either side. For example, being a longtime customer or acquaintance of the other side.

The preemptory challenges are fewer. The lawyer gives no reason and does not have to explain why. The jurors are questioned four at a time to choose or excuse. In some states on civil cases, the jurors are of six people. But not for this trial. There would be twelve.

Actually, as the jurors were being chosen, Tyler became involved and his intensity calmed somewhat.

Jamie told him, "Don't drink so much water, you'll slosh."

And Tyler replied, "Right."

It was especially interesting for Tyler to watch another lawyer question the potential jurors. One guy seemed so helpful and nice. And Jamie used a pre-emptory challenge to get rid of him.

With curiosity, Tyler asked Jamie, "Why not he?"

"I saw him talking kindly to a cousin of the bastard."

Tyler nodded. "I hadn't known the other side were bastards."

"You'll learn."

So, eventually, the jury was settled and the trial began. To be one of such a trial is very limiting to their thinking. They are immersed in all the ramifications of witness examinations and cross-examinations. They have to keep track of who has said what all. And use it or hide it.

Jamie and Tyler did win. That was supposed to be because of their research and the reputation of the Andersons. But who knows how the wind will blow?

Jamie and Tyler did a sterling job of it. And they were used up with the end of it. Tyler made no bones about it. He said, "Wow. I watched that jury the whole entire time, and they listened and watched so closely and were so solemn and serious. I had no idea which way they'd go. I thought our witnesses were perfect. I thought your questions were germane. And you presented them just right."

Even Jamie admitted to being wrung out. But he was past that trial and looking at another.

"How can you switch so easily?" Tyler asked with squinched eyes.

"You'll get used to it."

But Tyler took the afternoon off and went to his apartment. He wanted quiet. Peace. Time to let his brain relax.

So what did he do? He put on a workout rig and went jogging. He ran four miles. He came back to the apartment. There, he listened to the messages. And Kayla was one who had called. She said, "You did a great job! Congratulations!"

And Tyler stripped, went into the bath for a shower, dried himself, punched the mute button on the phone and went to bed—and slept. Out. Dreamless. Rejuvenation. He didn't hear anything, he was so deep in exhausted sleep.

Eight

So the next thing Tyler tried clearing out was his
office. Having done his apartment so well, he realized
it had been simple compared to his portion of the
office. Jamie's side was rather tamed. It was Tyler's
desk that was obscene. The only pristine thing on his
desk was his computer.

It was their office file cabinets that would be a
chore. He dreaded it all, but he was committed.

He faced the fact that he was reluctant in getting
started on something so mental and physical that
would take a long time. There were too many files.
Most were in a room of their own. It would take a
lot of decisions and time. He found he was hesitating.

Discipline. Yeah. That old, nasty word. It had been
ground into him all his human life.

Those last words caught his attention. His—human—life? And he considered the subconscious se-

lection of that word. Did that mean he could have been subhuman? Prehuman? Antihuman? Another form entirely?

As fascinating as the lure of it was, the human Tyler didn't allow his imagination to narrow his attention into the lure. To define the human or whatever other thing he might be could take all his free time and library research just to satisfy his curiosity.

He needed to be geared, concentrated and get the damned files in control. Yes.

He did sigh and take another mental glance at such a fascinating slip of his subliminal dip.

But he had decided he would do his desk first. So he began on straightening out and discarding all the junk and files he had gathered in and around his desk. He stayed late. It wasn't too bad. It took some evening time that week. Since he was back to batching it, he really had nothing else to do to entertain himself.

Some of the papers needed to be filed, and he put them in a hold tray to get that done when he did the file cabinets. While he was not a neophyte with file cabinets, he wasn't that comfortable with them.

One of the office staff asked him, "Do you need help in filing those?"

Tyler replied, "No. It's good discipline. Another time would be great, but now this is an underline of the need not to put things off."

The staff person smiled. "Holler if you need help."

And Tyler said, "Thank you."

As he worked along, his mind branched off in a portion with the time to debate if he was maturing. Perhaps. He was being very adult with Kayla. His rigid self-discipline was amazing even to him!

He'd been astounded and his sex had been stunned when he'd let her go. Godzilla had gone berserk and wild. He'd noted that. But his sex had been furious and saw to it that he had suffered.

He looked down at the bulge in his trousers. Silently, he said to it, *Cut it out, I know how you feel!*

It didn't let up. It just went on wanting and agitating. So Tyler pulled out his shirt and let the tails cover the damned, stubborn part of him that he couldn't control.

How could a man love the neediness only when he wanted it? Ah, the sweet pain of such suffering.

It took almost a week to get his desk in order. Of course, the file bin was larger, but it was separate and he knew why the papers should be kept in the office files instead of lost on his desk, and he knew where they would be put.

He labeled them exactly and put them aside to be filed another time. He looked at his desk.

He sat down and observed the ordered top. The files that were current and in sequence were in the top drawer. He had the entire desk under control. It was a heady feeling of accomplishment.

And he observed the stack of papers to be filed. They were separated, in order and alphabetized.

Tyler lay back in his office chair. He hadn't had this feeling of being in control in a long, long time. And he had to smile. In control…of paper?

So he got up, turned off the lights and left. His car was one of the few left in the parking garage. He got in and drove to their—to *his* apartment. That pristine apartment.

He parked in his apartment slot, walked into the

building and down the hall. He opened the door of his place and stood, eyeing the tidiness. The gleaming surfaces. Of course, he knew that the drawers were neat. Everything was in control. His control.

He wondered if the time would ever come that he could tidy up Kayla and be in control of her? If he could conquer the paper in his office, he could surely conquer her. Right? Naw. The papers had no brain nor could they move themselves.

And he thought of all the lost papers and wondered if they actually could move? Could they sneak away? How?

He showered. And he went to the neat and tidy bed and slept the sleep of any hungry man. He tore the bed apart in his sleep with his wild dreams. She was always just beyond him, and there were always other men interfering.

She did lure other eyes. She was an alluring woman. She lured him.

He wakened sweating in that linen mess and looked at the dark ceiling quite soberly. Why would he allow anyone to interfere with his life as she was doing? All that it took was self-discipline.

He was the Captain of his ship and the Master of his soul.

Of course.

He got up, tidied the bed and went into the bathroom. He put a warm cloth on his hot face and wiped off all the sweat. He took off his pajamas and went back to bed naked. And he slept.

So it was the next morning that he went into his office and his filing tray was gone. He was shocked. Who had taken the tray? He looked at Jamie's casual desk. The missing papers were not there. He asked Jamie, "Did you see my tray for filing?"

Not looking up, Jamie said, "Susan took it."

If Jamie didn't look up, how did he know who had it? That made Tyler indignant. He inquired with calm, "Why would she take it?"

Never looking up, Jamie replied, "It was ready for filing, she files, she took it and it's all probably already filed."

"Oh." There was nothing else for Tyler to say. It just made more stuff he'd have to check out in the files. He was ticked. Someone—in this case, Susan—should have inquired what he wanted done with those papers.

Tyler opened his tidy brief and began to research a trial in which they were involved. They probably wouldn't go into court. If there was a trial, it could be assigned to someone else.

But after supper, when Tyler went back to the office to begin on the file cabinets, he was startled to find them as neat and organized as they could be. He had never really been in the files to actually check them out. He told a clerk what he wanted and it was there on his desk.

But the files were updated and organized. It was a cross between relief and disappointment. The relief came before the disappointment. There was more of the relief.

So...his evening was free.

He went to the local bar to see if anyone was around. It was loosely inhabited by some locals. Tyler knew them by sight. They lifted their hands to recognize him, and he nodded in reply. No one included him. He'd never been with any of them before, so they didn't expect him to join them. They only acknowledged him.

Some woman came along and asked, "Lonesome?"

"Nah. Thanks, anyway."

She hesitated, but he didn't look up or say anything so she went off along the bar.

Tyler didn't finish the beer. He went out of the bar and down the street to the parking garage for his car. And he drove over to his parents' house. They were watching something on their humongous TV and were only peripherally glad to see him and shifted their chairs enough for him to be included.

He sat down and was sorry. Their taste in politicians was different. He didn't care for the man or his manner of speaking. He was a sham. His indignation was a lie. It had no foundation.

Tyler endured him for as briefly as he could before he got up and got a beer. All his siblings were gone. Some permanently, but those still around weren't there.

He paced around but his parents didn't catch his restlessness so he drifted off and went to his empty apartment. He watched Looney Tunes as the only tolerable thing to watch. That didn't last long.

He put on his jogging duds and went out to run. He was grateful running was a habit of so many people. He was accepted as was. He ran easily and it helped.

How strange that he was disappointed because the files were already tidied. Any business keeps the files current. The law offices have old files in the basement in case something could be gleaned from them. But the rest of the file cabinets were obviously kept tidy and up-to-date.

That was nice. Why hadn't he known?

He'd never inquired.

He paced around the apartment. Then he did what he'd obviously wanted to all along and he called Kayla.

She answered her phone, and Tyler listened to her voice. It was ordinary and not at all smoky or luring. He gently hung up. He didn't know what to say to her anyway. He'd just stumble his words around and sound like an idiot.

He'd hardly hung up when his phone rang. Because it was a private number, he answered, "Yeah?"

Kayla said, "How come you hung up? Call the wrong number?"

And he asked, "How'd you know it was me?"

She replied easily, "I have a caller ID, and I remember our old number."

"Are you okay?" He asked that.

"Sure."

"You sound...quiet."

She replied quietly, "There's nothing to celebrate."

"We won our last case."

"I saw it."

He was astonished. So much so that his voice was very vulnerable as he asked softly, "You were there?"

"Not all the time. But I got to see your cross examination. You did a very good job of it. The jurors listened and took you very seriously."

"Thank you."

"It reminded me of your first trial. You were a basket case until you got into court, and you smoothed out and seemed very calm and sure."

"I was."

She assured him, "You did very well with this one. I was proud of you."

"Thank you."

"So were your parents."

Tyler exclaimed softly, "*They* were there?"

In his ear, her voice was positive as she explained, "It was a big case. Your dad said if you didn't win after that cross examination, he was going to go get his Thunder Boom out after the jury." Thunder Boom was what the kids had called Mr. Fuller's duck gun.

"Have you ever gone duck hunting? It seems to me Dad promised to take you out. Did he?"

"We've gone about five times in these last two years."

Tyler gasped, "Five times? He's only taken me once!"

"You're probably not good company."

And Tyler turned vulnerable. "Was that why you left?"

"You took me to the most—" she sought the words "—remarkable places."

"Which ones were those?"

"You misunderstand. I didn't *like* the places you thought were so interesting."

"The dogfight." It was a statement. He didn't need to guess. "That wasn't planned. We just went to see what all those cars were doing there."

"Yes. I was appalled."

"Obviously. You're not at all subtle. How come you went off without me?"

And she said snidely, "With those big dogs, there wasn't any room for—another—animal."

"I'm a human man. I'm not an animal."

"Then why did you want to go to such a place where the dogs had no choice?"

And he told the phone quite seriously, "I was curious as to why all those cars were there."

"I've never considered you as such a person. You'd always been the hero until we blundered into that dogfight."

"You rejected me for one dogfight? I left almost as soon as you did. When I finally got home, you were asleep but the four dogs growled at me."

"I was appalled by the dogfights."

So he was logical. "You wouldn't have bought those four dogs and freed them if we *hadn't* gone there."

"That's true. Thank you for them."

And he asked a very urgent question, "Didn't being there and seeing it widen your knowledge of the world and the people in it?"

Dryly, she informed him, "I could have done without the knowledge."

"Did you see how the people there loved what they saw? Did you see their sparkling eyes and hear their laughter?"

"Did any of them know the dogs who died in the fights?"

"I doubt it. They just bet on which one will win. And there's a whole lot more dogs in the world than you'd ever know. At least if you walk the streets."

Tersely, she snapped, "I have a job." Even in his ear, her voice was stilted. "I don't have to walk the streets."

"Whoa. What do you mean by that? I was talking about exercise on streets where dogs live. You have to watch where you run or jog."

"Oh. Yes." She agreed. "You're right. I don't know why people in the city have dogs."

"Why does anyone? They like the animals, and the dogs are friendly and interested in the world. They will even watch TV with the humans."

She thought of the TV show and asked, "Lassie?"

"I suppose." Then he asked, "Who all bought the dogs from you?"

"Tom Keeper."

"All four?" His voice was hostile.

"No. He just has friends who help out. They took the dogs and passed them on to other people. They found good places for them. Only one dog didn't settle in. Tom took him out to the far ranch and showed him the prairie dog holes proliferating in one corner of his land."

Tyler inquired, "The dog took over?"

"Actually, from what Tom says, the dog is fascinated. He digs, too, but he gets nowhere. The tunnels are mostly lure. The dog gets the wrong ones. And it's very frustrating."

Tyler inquired, "So he's in therapy?"

She laughed. "Probably, soon. Tom thinks it's excellent training for the dog. Of course, at first the paws were scraped badly and the dog had to wear soft leather boots for a while."

"Now how would a dog be talked into wearing boots?"

"Tom let him lick them off a couple of times and walk on the abraded paws. Then he would put the boots back on the dog and take him for a walk. It took a while, but the dog gradually allowed Tom to take care of him, and he wore the boots until he was healed. By then he knew to watch cautiously, and eventually, he got one of the prairie dogs."

And softly, into the phone mouthpiece, Tyler had the gall to say a soft "Ahhhh" of sympathy.

However Kayla was snide. "Don't give me such a compassionate sound. You took me to that dogfight."

"I had no idea it *was* a dogfight." Tyler was ticked. He said, "A little prairie dog and a great big old dog are two different things."

So she informed the city boy, "Those prairie dogs have a tunnel system that grows with the expansion of the mass. They proliferate quite rapidly. They ruin good soil. Nothing grows there because they eat the roots."

Tyler was profound, "You protect big, mean dogs and commit the lives of darling little prairie—"

"Oh, be quiet! You don't know anything about the prairie dogs. They're a nuisance!"

With some exasperation, he asked, "How can you be compassionate to fighting dogs and think prai—"

While he couldn't see it through the phone, she still waved one hand in irritation. "There *is* no comparison! How could you have taken me to such a place?"

And vulnerable, he told her into the phone's mouthpiece, "I wanted to see what was drawing all those people there. I looked. It's why I found a phone booth on the road and called the authorities to stop it."

She was silent. Then she told him, "You're a superior man. You—"

"You think I'm...superior?"

And she said, "You're aware of that. You know

your potential. You're not only curious, you want to help. You throw yourself into anything and—"

And he interrupted strongly, "That was why I wanted to see the dogfights! You can't make a charge if you aren't a witness."

She huffed, "You could have *asked* if I *wanted* to stay there!"

"You'd have refused!" He told her in surprised logic.

"Of course!" she shouted.

And he elaborated with intensity, "But you would have missed being witness to a happenstance experience!"

"Good gravy, Tyler, why would I want to *experience* such a brutal thing?"

He told her, "You love fights between men."

"Well, they know what they're doing and they choose to do it. With dogfights they just have a bitch in heat that stimulates the males into challenging the other dogs."

With compassion, Tyler said kindly, "Life isn't easy for males."

"Oh, for Pete's sake!"

"What would you do...what would you have done if some other woman had wanted me?"

And in a sour voice, Kayla said, "Trilby."

That boggled Tyler and he questioned, "Trilby? Who's Trilby?"

"That witch who tried to shove me aside so she could have you. Remember her?"

"Some other woman—wanted me?" He was astonished.

And with derision, Kayla snorted. "You never guessed?"

"I was so taken with you that I couldn't *see* any other woman. You say there was somebody who... wanted me?"

"I did."

"I meant some *other* woman."

She asked in a hostile way, "Why would you look beyond me?"

"I didn't."

And she dusted it off. She mentioned yet again, "You divorced me."

"Kayla, Kayla, you know damned good and well that I didn't want a divorce. You were neglecting me. I filed to get your attention. You let me go ahead. You ignored me."

She snorted. "Men are so pushy."

He questioned in a hostile manner, "Who's been pushy with you? Just give me his name."

"No man."

"A *woman's* after you?" He was shocked.

"No, idiot."

"No idiot is after you so it's somebody that's—"

"*You* are the idiot."

"Now, how in the world could you make such a decision? You haven't even been around me enough in the last year to know whether or not I can behave like an adult. I can."

"I'll have to check this out."

"Come over for supper tomorrow." That sounded casual enough, but he'd ignored his own gasp before he said the words.

Kayla had heard it and she smiled. Since they were on the phone, he didn't see the smile. Sometimes it's just best to talk to a man over the phone so he doesn't leap to any odd conclusions.

She said, "No, thank you. I want to go to the club."

"Oh. Okay. What time? I need to get reservations."

And she replied, "Next to the dance floor."

He admitted, "I'm not the greatest dancer in the world."

"You did Mrs. Gates's sessions okay. I know that's true because I was a level below you, being so much younger, and I saw you dancing. At that time you couldn't talk and dance at the same time."

"I've learned to just move back and forth first on one foot and then on the other so that it seems like we're dancing, but we can talk."

She said, "I know."

He was disappointed. "I thought I'd been real sly with that."

"You're sly in a lot of things, but a dancer has a lot of problems if he just sways back and forth."

"That way I get to concentrate on y—the lady."

"Who else have you been dancing with lately?"

"Oh," he lied. "There've been a couple of partners. Old friends." He diminished it all, saying, "Nothing serious." He knew that would tick her curiosity.

While it did tick her curiosity, it irritated the very liver out of her. She asked bluntly, "Who." It was a lead-in and not a question.

"Well, let's see. There was that redhead down at the men's bar by the river. And—"

"A *red*head?" She had gasped that out without realizing how jealous it sounded. But who can compete with a *redhead?*

Tyler silently smiled into his phone. Kayla loved

him. All he had to do was make her realize it enough for her to tell that to him. He said to her, "She probably dyes her hair. The roots looked a little light. She's probably gray-haired."

Some men are especially crafty. They know when to say what to a woman. Tyler had just said three such sentences exactly right to Kayla. Some men are gentlemen and never say unkind things to a wife or ex-wife about a competitive woman. They're dumb.

So Kayla didn't hang up but went on talking to Tyler and listening. Actually, it was the first time in their rather short acquaintance that they'd exchanged as many thoughts and opinions.

The two talked for a long while. Their voices got sleepy, and he heard her yawn. He finally yawned almost silently, and she said, "Good heavens! Look at the time!" But she was pleased he'd been talking to her for so long.

He said sleepily, "You ought to be here in your own bed."

"Only half of it was mine."

"I wouldn't...crowd you. It would just be nice to have you—close."

She almost said a snippy reply, but instead she said a soft, "Good night."

"'nite, honey. It was nice to talk to you."

She was silent for a while and then she gently hung up the phone.

Thoughtfully, Tyler got up from the bed and began to undress. His sex leaped out of his underwear, and Tyler sighed in sympathy. Mentally, he'd called it Godzilla from the time he was fourteen.

He'd never mentioned the naming to any of his

male friends. He thought their reaction would not be positive, but their hilarity would smother him. And which ones would keep the name to himself? None of them. Word would have spread through the entire male population of San Antonio and on beyond until it had leaked out to other cities then to other states and foreign countries and *every*body would have known.

Women never know what all a man has to endure. That's why men are strong and silent. They've fought or threatened so many dissidents, and they don't dare to tell *any*thing or it'll be zinging around the circuit in the next hour!

Tyler took a cold shower and went to bed. He was already tired and it was late, so he did sleep...mostly. Of course, he wakened and the bed was again torn apart. Rumpled? He'd been restless.

Tyler went to the office the next morning on time, as usual, and Jamie observed his approach. Jamie had turned his chair and watched Tyler enter the room and go to his desk. Since their shared office was not all that big, it didn't take Tyler long to finish the goal.

Jamie asked kindly, "What the hell's the matter with you?"

Tyler looked at his friend with cold eyes. He enunciated clearly, "Nothing."

"You look like you've been pulled through a knothole."

"I've cleaned ou—my apartment, and I've organized my desk."

"And you've found there is a crew who files things that are backups. Your computer works miracles and you look like hell. What's the matter with you? Are you sick?"

Tyler nodded as he turned on his computer and shifted the newly laid papers on his desk. He told Jamie, "I'm sick of being hassled by overlings who have no business at all of harassing me to entertain—himself." That narrowed down the overling.

Jamie considered Tyler. Then he said gently, "I beg your pardon."

"I forgive you."

"We're due to go with Mr. Reardon to a conference. He believes it will stimulate you."

Tyler asked, "Not you?"

"I get to go along. Mr. Reardon didn't want anyone to think he is singling you out for attention."

"He wants *me* to experience this?"

"He's a little sentimental about you. First Kayla and now this trial. He thinks you were brilliant."

With some indignation, Tyler protested, "You were in charge of the whole shebang!"

And Jamie smiled. He told Tyler, "Barb thinks I'm brilliant. That's enough for me. But he thinks you will become the fairhaired boy and brilliant. That's one hell of a burden on anyone, and I gladly give you that spotlight. Good luck."

"Aw,—!"

Jamie laughed. His eyes sparkling with his humor, he told Tyler, "I wouldn't trade knowing you for any other guy in this entire organization. I don't know of another man who is so brilliant in law who is also so normal. You're okay."

And it was that compliment which Tyler held to his heart as a token of worth. With that confidence, he might convince Kayla to reconsider him.

Would she?

Who ever knew what a woman would do or think or wear? They were such strange creatures. God probably made them that way so that men couldn't be bored. Men spent most of their time trying to figure out what they'd said wrong or why she wanted that?

Well, female bodies sure felt good up against a man's. It had been almost a year by then since the divorce. That was sure as hell a long dry spell. And Godzilla urgently agreed.

Nine

So Tyler and Kayla talked on the phone. He didn't try to push it. He didn't beg her to come back to him. They were getting acquainted again. It took a lawyer to realize that while they'd been sexually intense, they really hadn't known each other very well.

For a couple their ages, now twenty-eight and twenty-five, their lust had led them into a rather quick marriage. Now they were beginning to know each other over the phone. Separated that way, without the intimate allure, they could concentrate more on getting to know each other's thinking. Their opinions.

She asked, "How did the filing go?"

"I found out they have a whole section in the firm of filers. They tidy up the files and find those needed, and I hadn't realized what all the different sections of the firm do. I know about the secretarial pool, but I hadn't paid any attention to how much filing was done. With the computers, you can pull up just about anything, but if we ever lost the computer files, we still have the real files.''

''Ummm.'' That was agreement but obviously she was not terribly interested in the subject of filing.

He said, ''We have baseball on Thursday. Want to go?''

''Maybe.''

And he was smart enough not to push for her commitment.

They talked about mutual friends and discussed what those people were doing and how they were getting along. How interesting it was that they, who were divorced, could be critical of other couples.

Actually, they gossiped. She knew everything about everyone, and he was interested and exclaimed in shock.

She asked with curiosity, ''Now why would you be surprised by John doing that?''

''John's always seemed so stable. Maybe I ought to talk to him?''

''How are you going to convince John to make up with Connie when you've divorced me?''

''John'll understand.''

''*John* will? He's off the *wall!*''

But as Kayla had mentioned that Tyler had divorced her, Tyler could hardly say anything about his knowing women. Connie was an airhead. Actually, John would be better off without her. He'd talk to John and see how he really felt.

Kayla asked, ''Would you like to go out tramping this weekend?''

He was silent as he controlled his shock. *She had*

asked him to meet with her! To be with her! Together!
He said, "Oh—okay."

"I'll bring something to eat. Could you bring the drinks?"

He'd take 100 Proof whiskey and get her drunk! He'd seen her drunk once. Her heavy eyelids. Her flopping hands. He knew how she'd be after drinking that dynamite. She'd be unable to control him, and he'd just go ahead.

He said in a rather husky voice, "I'd be glad to bring the drinks. What would you suggest?" He'd let her choose, but for the picnic, he'd take the wicked stuff. And, shucks, out there in the boondocks, in the thirsty day, that would be all they'd have to drink!

Into his ear against the phone, Kayla suggested, "Cokes...7-UP? Something like that?"

"I'll see what they have." Sure he would. His feet turned into hooves and his ears changed, elongating, and little horns began to sprout from his skull poking through the skin on his scalp and into his hair. He smiled.

It was then that Godzilla enunciated, *"Uuuuhhhhh. No."*

Godzilla said *that?*

And Tyler felt Godzilla shrug as he said, *Later.*

In all that time, Kayla said she'd get back to Tyler after she found out where they could tramp.

Tyler agreed, "Okay." And they hung up their phones. Tyler sat there thinking. Well, hell. And mentally, Tyler made some excessively critical and sneering remarks to his phantom creature who was his libido, Godzilla.

Godzilla said, *Shame on you!*

It is disillusioning to have one's counterself take

up the flag of purity that way. And snidely, Tyler told Godzilla, "It's your loss." And he half-closed his eyes in a mean way as he waited for the response of his sex.

But instead of razzing the host of his being, Godzilla sighed in regret and just said, *We know!*

What can a man do whose very sex has empathy for the man? And strict rules for behavior? Something he'd called...Godzilla?

So it was all thrown back into Tyler's lap. And it was right there that Godzilla lived.

In a rather nasty way, Tyler said mentally, "I believe I'll change your name. You've gotten beyond the Godzilla stage, and you're a wimp. I shall call you Wimp."

There was no reply.

Slowly, Tyler realized that the name fit not his sex, but *him!* He needed to be more aggressive with his ex-wife who had divorced him. Well, actually, he had divorced *her,* but she had never even once protested or questioned or anything!

So he and she were going out tramping. She would tell him where. She would scare off everybody from some vacant land, and she'd molest him and ravish him just for practice.

Okay.

He could handle that. And he thought what an available handle Wimp was. The Wimp was already puffed up and ready at the very idea of being molested. How does a man keep his sex under control? Who is in charge? Who has control?

And Tyler knew it was all his own responsibility. If he didn't take the Wimp out of his pants, it would have to behave...enough. Kayla was safe.

The very idea of a safe Kayla sent Tyler into a decline.

So on the next day, Tyler had begun another case concerning a will. When someone with money dies, there are people who will contest the will, if they aren't on it. Or if they are, they're positive they ought to get more money. They then will file a petition with Probate Court to set the will aside.

There would be other people who complained they were due money and/or property.

They said the deceased was incompetent or under the influence of others. A mistress was supposedly promised caretaking. The remnants of the family rejected such a thing. They said she was pushy trash.

So Tyler was to interview all those people, question the deceased's relatives and verify who owned what. He'd be checking banks, interviewing and taking notes besides going through papers.

Having committed himself to interfering, Tyler called his friend John for lunch at a Mexican restaurant down by the man-made newest river loop.

John responded sourly, "Okay. Your treat." And he hung up.

Tyler replaced the phone slowly. His head tilted as he considered that perhaps Connie had good *reason* not to want John around? Hmmmm.

At noon, a disgruntled Tyler went through the building and off down the street. Being a Good Samaritan wasn't all that much fun or satisfying. He went into the restaurant and, fortunately, had reservations. He sat down and waited.

John drifted in eventually. He was sullen and didn't give one damn that he was late. He stood and looked around, and Tyler stood up so that John could see him. Tyler thought he really ought to have turned his back to John and hidden.

John came over to the table, didn't reply to Tyler's greeting but just sat down. He told the waitress he'd have a beer.

Tyler smiled at the waitress and said in Spanish, "Not now, maybe not at all. Bring us two enchiladas each—and say the beer will be along. You can *say* right away. Please."

And she replied smoothly in Spanish the equivalent of, "You got it."

Since the restaurant was ready for the lunch crowd, the silent two did not have to wait long for their lunch. It was delivered within ten minutes.

In the silence between them, John continued to glare around for the waitress as Tyler began to eat. John jerked his head around as he watched for and finally spotted her. She was clear across the room. He tried to nab another, but they had all been tipped off and each smiled, held up one finger and replied in Spanish, "one minute" and vanished.

Tyler decided that just being with John was enough for that time. He would simply be there. Ignored company. In the silence, Tyler ate the enchilada with hungry relish. He used the crisp pieces of tortillas to scoop up the chili gravy that was laced with melted cheese. He made appreciating sounds.

Now who can resist that sort of cleverness?

So John had a bite. He had another. He used the tortilla scoops also. He watched for a waiter.

A man in a white apron came to the table with two

bottles and glasses. He said with smiling distress, "We have no actual beer. This is a substitute and better for the businessman. It tastes—ah. There is no lingering breath. Try it. It's on the house."

With interest, Tyler poured his fake beer into a glass. Silently, he tasted it. His head nodded as he licked his lips thoughtfully. He smiled and had another sip. He never once looked at John. He went back to eating.

John still searched for a waiter but those who zipped by smiled and said, "one minute" in Spanish and disappeared. By then John had eaten one of the enchiladas and he'd had a glass of the fake beer. He looked at it thoughtfully. He still did not speak to Tyler.

Patiently, looking casually around, Tyler waited until John was finished with his lunch. Tyler was relaxed and silent. He noted other people. He lifted a hand now and again to greet someone he knew. An old friend stopped by and Tyler greeted him. And he introduced John to the man.

John brusquely acknowledged the introduction and went on eating. And the visitor ignored the rudeness, chatted cheerily with Tyler and then moved on.

During all that silent while, Tyler decided this would be the last time he'd ever see John. But then he considered that John could be suffering. Tyler realized that he was needed just for the companionship. He couldn't allow an old acquaintance to suffer alone. He was committed to this abusive silence. John suffered. He was a human. Tyler was committed.

When John had finished eating, he was still looking for a waiter for real beer. No one came. He was disgruntled, and he continued silent.

Tyler moved his chair back a little and looked at John. If John didn't go back to his office, Tyler realized he'd stay with him. This apparently was a crucial day of some kind.

It was Tyler who paid the bill and he wrote: *Thank you!* on the bottom. They went out of the restaurant door and stood in the sun. Tyler said, "Let's go down to the river walk and go that way back?"

John stood there.

Tyler moved a little in that direction. Then he looked back, and John sighed with such irritation but he followed. So Tyler set his pace to match John's slow one.

The San Antonio river walk is the product originally of the Work Projects Administration under President Franklin D. Roosevelt in the 1930s. Each stair up to the street is different.

The river walk has been such a pleasure for everyone that more man-made river loops have been added. There are riverboats and sidewalks along the river loops. There are all sorts of shops, an open-air theater and places to dine, or snack. There are a great many hotels built along the river loops.

It was a pleasant place to be. Tyler knew the walks well, and he ambled along not appearing to guide John. He talked into his fold-up cellular phone. He called in to his office and told Jamie he'd be delayed. He was with John. Jamie said, "You're a smart man. Good luck."

And Tyler called in to John's office.

John's secretary said very seriously, "Good for you."

Tyler and John walked silently. Tyler took off his

tie and slid it into his pocket. He opened his shirt a couple of buttons. He breathed the sweet TEXAS air.

John was silent.

So was Tyler.

They found a bench in the shade and sat down. Tyler was still silent. He was simply—there. However, it was fascinating and riveting to Tyler that *so was John*...there! Would he talk? Could he get the bile of bitterness out of himself?

And would Tyler have the brain to be silent enough or if needed, would he know what to say?

The TEXAS wind was gentle. It stirred their hair. It touched their faces and it was alive. The fragrance of clean air is special. Was the clean air from the filtering of all the trees? Or was it that the smog had been eliminated?

Tyler watched the patterns of the leaves shading the sun's light. The day was another perfect day in San Antonio. It was accepted that was so. When it rained, it was a gift of change.

John said, "It was two years ago today."

Uh-oh. It wasn't John's temper, it was his grief? Should he ask John what had happened? It wasn't the divorce. That was only about five months ago. What had happened two years ago?

The only encouragement was that Tyler turned his head slowly and looked at John.

There were tears on John's cheeks. That about ruined Tyler, right there. He watched, his compassion growing.

"We lost a baby who was so new. And they said Connie shouldn't try again. I saw the baby. It was a little embryo. A tiny beginning baby. It didn't have a chance."

Without any notice, Tyler's mouth asked, "Is that why you two divorced?"

"No. She wanted a baby, and I wouldn't do it. She got mad at me. I was stubborn. I love her. But she cried because she wanted to try for one, and I wouldn't let her."

"You ought to go to our doctor."

"Your family doctor?"

"Kayla's and mine."

"You two getting back together?"

"Well, no."

"Dumb."

"Now, John. How can you say something like that about *us?*"

John's eyes were bloodshot from his tears. "You don't understand. But you two ought to be together. You were dumb to try the divorce trick. She let you go through with it."

"So you knew I didn't want a divorce. I was just trying to get her attention for—"

"It was stupid."

"Yeah." Then Tyler asked, "You ever see Connie?"

"Not very often. I can't get her phone number."

"I'll ask Kayla."

John looked at Tyler with his tear red eyes. "Would she give it to you?"

Very gently, Tyler told his friend, "I'll be subtle."

John frowned. "In what way?"

"I'll just say I need to contact her."

John flopped back and spread his knees wide in disgust. "That's about the dumbest thing I can think of for you to do. You'll just make Kayla so curious that she'll call Connie and ask what's going on."

Tyler frowned at the perfect sky and said, "That's true. Women do that."

And after a time of silence, John said, "When God gave us women, why did He have to make them like they are?"

And Tyler sighed before he replied, "Hell, how do I know? He thought they'd stimulate us? They're more annoying than stimulating. How could God have fouled up like that?"

"He hadn't made any women before then," John explained, "It was probably just an experiment. Or He wanted to distract us?"

"Women are a serious puzzle. I filed for divorce from Kayla, and she didn't do *one* thing about it!"

"I know."

Tyler poured it out. "All I wanted was her attention. Her concern. And she let me go!"

John shook his head. "I don't understand women. I couldn't believe Connie would divorce me just because I wouldn't let her have a baby." He looked at Tyler with his red, leaking eyes. "I only wanted her."

"Did you tell her that?"

"Well, hell, I told her she wasn't going to have any kids at all!"

"Maybe she thought you were being critical of her not having kids."

"I told her I loved her more than any kid."

Tyler's eyes began to redden. "Women are so strange."

"Yeah. Let's go get a drink."

Tyler sighed hugely. "Naw. That's no solution. We have to think and discuss and figure out women. Then we'll decide how to cope with Connie. After we solve that, maybe you two can help me with Kayla. Women are such a nuisance! But we don't have any other choice.''

"I know.''

Tyler looked around. It was such a beautiful day. The breeze was so gentle and kind. Why couldn't a woman be like that?

The two disgruntled men sat silently and considered all the people in the world and all the problems. It was depressing to consider. Nobody really got anything solved. The whole world population just proliferated, still quarreling, still breeding and still fighting each other.

Out of the silence, Tyler asked, "Why don't you invite her to lunch tomorrow?''

.''You inviting Kayla?''

"Kayla?'' Tyler was startled. "Okay. I'll ask her.''

"You get her nailed down and—''

"She'll resist that.''

"I mean you get her committed, and then I'll tackle Connie.''

"That's fair.''

There was another silence. Then John asked, "You ready to go back to work? I really don't have all this time to give to you.''

Tyler was startled. *John* had been concerned for *him?* Tyler couldn't think of any response at all. So he said, "Okay.''

And John stood up. "Try Kayla again. She might be ready to forgive you the divorce.''

"Well, that was just a warning thing and not serious.''

And the sage said kindly, "It was a hell of a shock to her. Ease up and let her talk to you and help you figure out what the hell you're doing.''

So with inner shock, Tyler said, "Thank you for your time today."

"I'm a good friend. If you ever need somebody again, wait a while. I can't give this much time just off the cuff this way. Take care of yourself. Call me anytime. I mean that. I'm always available to an old friend."

And the shocked Tyler soberly nodded his head.

The two climbed to the street and lifted their hands to each other as they separated and strode off to their offices.

Back at his desk, Tyler exclaimed to Jamie, "John thought he was baby-sitting *me!*"

Jamie actually looked up blankly. "How's that?"

And Tyler said, "I thought I was giving *him* time to open his pus-filled soul and clear it off, and *he* thought I needed *him!*"

Jamie grinned. "I'm glad he thought that. He might then think about himself. It's good for a man who has problems to understand there are other people who have problems."

"It'll be a while before I get over the amazement of this afternoon."

"It'll clean your soul, and you'll call Kayla and straighten out your lives."

Vulnerable, Tyler said, "She's very leery of me. I don't think she'd try again. But we are going on a picnic this weekend."

"Oh? Want Barbara and me along?"

Tyler pulled his rolling desk chair up into place as he said a positive, "No."

And Jamie chided, "I'll bet your mother ground it into you to say, 'No, *thank you.*'"

Tyler lifted his head and looked at the picture of one of the early partners on the wall. He squinted his eyes and said, "That has a familiar sound to it."

Back to looking at his papers, Jamie advised, "Practice."

Tyler exclaimed, "She said that, too. It was the piano."

Jamie exclaimed, "You play the piano?"

"Brilliantly. It's what switched me to the computer when I was fourteen. Mother was so amazed by the new personal Apple computers that she bought me one, and she encouraged me to use it. We didn't even have a printer until the Gorilla Banana came along with the matrix print."

"I remember those days."

"Look at the computers we have now."

Jamie was distracted by his papers, but he did say, "Incredible."

Like Jamie, Tyler was sucked in by the papers on his desk. He put what he needed into his computer and lost track of time.

Jamie never did.

But immersed in law, Tyler didn't have Jamie's particular mental touch with current things. When Tyler became involved, he lost touch with everything else.

He considered that. Maybe that was why Kayla had left him. He hadn't remembered to check in with her and listen. Hmmm. But the papers and interviews did intrude, and Tyler became embedded in law and was again lost to reality.

A deposition is like a cross-examination in Court in which the plaintiff or plaintiffs are sworn in. They are quizzed on allegations stated in a complaint that the Will should be set aside. Or it can be that the plaintiffs are not included in the Will or think they should have more than what was allotted in the Will.

People are fascinating.

But Tyler had set a time buzzer so that when it went off, he surfaced and understood it was Thursday and baseball was to be played. The reason he realized that was because he'd put a note beside the buzzer and that's what he saw as he stopped the damned intrusive buzzer.

If Tyler had a commitment of any kind, he used the buzzer to catch his attention. Tyler had to have an irritating, relentless buzzer because he could ignore anything else like a kinder, gentler one.

When Jamie was there in the office, he insisted on taking the part of the buzzer. He couldn't stand the blasted buzzer.

So that evening, about seven o'clock, the buzzer did go off. Tyler surfaced and saw there was a plate and salad bowl. Jamie must have done that. And Tyler had eaten it. Then he remembered he was supposed to play ball at eight.

He again saved the work he'd done on the computer and started the printer to print it all. He looked at his desk with regret but he was committed to playing baseball. Even he understood that it was best to get out and be with people. He could live, isolated, with his nose in law books.

A man can do that. So can a woman. They can be so engrossed in some distraction that they forget to know people. To see the sun set. To watch kids play. To see there are other people and there is a wide, wide world out there.

If they just look up to the horizon, that isn't bad.

At the baseball part of the park, Tyler looked at all the people in the stands and thought of their seeing the horizon. They were doing that. They'd come out to the park to visit and exchange ideas and call to others and watch the game and observe others kindly or with gossip. People need other people around.

And they need to look beyond their area to other peoples and to other horizons.

With the rest of the team, Tyler took to the field. He trotted out to second base and he looked up into the stands. He immediately saw Kayla and he waved.

She laughed and waved back.

He almost couldn't wipe the smile off his face during that game. He hit another home run! And his heart floated above him as he trotted around the bases and was sure his foot tromped on each and every base. He stood on home plate and laughed with his laughing, bunched up team crowding around him, shaking his hand, high fiving with hands, and bragging on him in the rough way of friends.

Exuberant, they said, "I've never seen a hit ball bounce on air thataway to get over a fence!" They said, "You can hit a ball!" "I had to see it to believe it!" And Tyler just laughed.

The people in the bleachers hollered and yelled so that Tyler had barely sat on the bench when the coach said he ought to give them a bow...forward. He was a humorist of a kind. So Tyler got up, bowed, took off his hat and waved it at Kayla. The cheering went on and Tyler had to laugh. How lucky he was. Not the run...just that Kayla was there.

With both hands high in the air so that he was sure to see her, Kayla laughed back at him.

Of course, *most* of his friends had both hands high in the air. But Tyler did see Kayla. If she'd actually been in the stands all those times she said she had, how had he missed her?

She hadn't waved? He hadn't seen her. It was probably because he hadn't believed she was actually there so he hadn't expected to see her.

He and the Wimp would see her that weekend. Yes. They'd go out into the countryside, they'd be together…and alone. Kayla. Was there any other woman in the world? No. Just Kayla.

If she turned him aside again, he'd probably become a recluse. A legal recluse. It wasn't all that unusual.

But there were others who chose that single life. Artists, musicians, scientists, writers, too many people who lived their lives in what they did and not ever looking up.

Later, sitting on the "dugout" bench, Tyler looked up into the stands. He didn't see all the others. Not even his family laughing down at him. He just saw Kayla. He smiled up at her. It took someone on his team to mention, "Uhhh, the inning's over, let's go. Hey, Tyler?"

And Tyler got up and trotted out to second base.

Ten

One thing about men. They know *every*thing that's going on. They say that women gossip. They shake their heads over such loose tongues. But when men are caught gossiping, they say adamantly that it is *not* gossip! They're just exchanging information!

While they were in the baseball "dugout," on the bench alongside the wire fence to first base, one of the guys said to Tyler, "I heard Tom Keeper's after your woman."

"Naw."

But another said slowly, moving carefully, "I heard it, too. You watch your back trail."

That meant Tyler ought to look behind him and be sure nobody was catching up to him...or to Kayla.

And another of the team told Tyler seriously, "That Tom Keeper will keep her. His family is thata-way...and so's *he*. As you can tell by the name they have, their habit goes a long way back in time. You watch out for him. He'll lure her with all that money."

"Yeah." That was said by about three or four others in an unpracticed and therefore nonsynchronized, vocal agreement.

So Tyler looked up in the stands. He wasn't looking for Kayla, he knew where she was. He was looking for that sneaky Tom Keeper.

Tom wasn't anywhere around Kayla. If he was there, he was hiding. That would be smart. And Tyler wondered, if it came to fisticuffs, could he beat Tom?

Tom was in pretty good condition.

One of the guys asked, "How did you let Kayla get away from you?"

And Tyler replied thoughtfully, "I don't rightly know. It just happened. I filed for divorce to panic her. I thought that would make her come running back home t—"

The hilarity cut him off. The guys exclaimed how stupid he was, and they agreed among themselves they needed to restructure his stupidity. They had no hope—at all—of him being anywhere *near* to intelligence, but they *might* could make a dent in his stupidity.

They about came apart with their laughter when Tyler replied seriously, "Maybe so."

One of the team, watching the game said, "I heard you was watching around some other woman. I don't recall her name."

Tyler responded, "Well, that was before we got married. I did look around. I did need to say goodbye to independence."

And another one of the team, standing, watching

the game closely, interrupted, "Her name wasn't Independence, it was Iowna."

Tyler said, "I'd forgotten about her!"

Another inquired with subtle knowledge, "Who in hell could forget Iowna?"

Someone else commented, "Well, when a guy's married to Kayla, other women just sorta fade away."

But George mentioned, "Kayla must be lonesome and needy, I'll call her for a date."

Tyler looked up at George and said, "I wouldn't do that if I was you."

And George slid his sleepy eyes over to Tyler and said, "If I was you—forty pounds lighter and six inches shorter—I wouldn't, either."

That was a sobering reality. George was indeed forty pounds heavier and six inches taller. Tyler told George, "Behave and don't be so snide or I'll get my mama to chastise you."

They loved it.

At the end of the game, Kayla waited in a group, each of whom she'd threatened with death if they left her there alone. She laughed and talked to them until Tyler came up by her. Then she flipped a dismissive hand at the others and said, "'bye."

The guys didn't leave. The women were honest and were willing to leave the two alone, but men tend to really irritate another man when he's courting. Especially, if the guy's courting Kayla. The women fooled the men. "I have the car keys, let's go."

"Uhhh," said George. "Hold it a minute."

And the sassy woman just glanced over her shoulder and swished her body in a shocking manner as she went on off...with George following willingly.

Women never pay any attention to the vital details of living. Nor will they allow a man to go ahead with what he's doing when she wants something else. They tend to control.

With the rest gone, Tyler asked the smile-licking, eye-catching woman in front of him, his ex-wife, "You going home with me?"

She looked surprised, as if she hadn't considered any such thing. She exclaimed, "That would be a good idea! I've been so curious if you've kept ah— the place tidy."

He watched her with a slight smile and was so engrossed that he didn't hear the calls from others who passed them.

Kayla did. She wiggled fingers and smiled. But she blushed and her body was restless.

Then her Davie parents came by, and stopped in the way of watchful parents. They exclaimed, "Well, hello, Tyler." They said it as if they were surprised to see the actual him...and had not realized until then the fact that he had played in the game.

They all spoke kindly. And they visited for a while. Then they said to Kayla, "You take Jim and Henrietta. They're on your way. Nice to see you, Tyler. That home run was perfect!"

Her daddy gave Tyler a friendly pat on his shoulder and smiled. Fathers *love* to louse up a daughter-courting male.

And with that brief encounter, the Davies and their friends went on off.

Tyler looked with some enduring patience at Jim and Kayla's apartment mate Henrietta.

Jim smiled at Tyler with twinkling eyes.

Hennie just smiled with lowered eyelids. She was

so amused. Parents of daughters have a way of sundering the plans of any male. Even divorced couples.

The four went to Tyler's car. Then Tyler had to wait, holding the car door until Jim got out of the front seat and into the back. In his hesitation to change seats, Jim explained logically, "The girls'll want to talk."

Standing there, holding the car door open, Tyler replied with rigidly harnessed patience, "They share an apartment, they don't need to talk together in the car. They can talk anytime. Get in back."

"Oh," Jim said as if assimilating the fact the two women were apartment mates. And he got out and changed seats with Kayla. Then Jim complained and bounced up and down because the seat he'd taken from Kayla was too hot for him to sit on.

While Hennie laughed, and so did Jim, Kayla only smiled with female patience of an immature male. But Tyler looked off to the distance as if inquiring of God why other humans were so stupid? He received no reply, but Tyler *thought* he heard a compassionate sigh.

It could have been the wind.

So Tyler drove the three to the girls' apartment. Jim got out. So did Tyler. Jim started Hennie up to the door and they talked comfortably.

However, not leaving the side of the car, Kayla turned to Tyler and said, "The home run was *great!* You're the best of the team."

Hennie heard and commented, "I love prejudice."

Jim told them, "This is the first season Tyler's hit a home run. It must be that he's free of the burden of a wife. Kayla, don't allow him—"

Tyler put in, "Go home. Walk. Or sit in the car."

Jim exclaimed, "Not escort my woman to the front door? Allow her to find her own way?"

Tyler said flatly, "I'll be with Kayla, we'll watch out for Henrietta."

Hennie gasped in comment, "The entire name! He's being formal."

Jim exclaimed, "So *that's* it! I knew there was some—"

Rather forcefully, Tyler said, "Hush!"

"Uh-oh," Jim told Hennie, "he's serious."

And Hennie directed, "Come along and leave them be."

Jim complained, "I didn't know if you'd feed me so I bought all those cold hot dogs and all that beer. You drank most of the beer. Are you excited and pliant?"

"No."

"Oh." Jim put his hands in his pockets and strolled along with Hennie to the apartment door.

With them far enough away, Kayla again said, "We have the picnic on Saturday."

And Tyler told her, "Knowing that is all that's keeping me going."

"I didn't know you liked picnics that much."

"Just recently."

And she said, "I see."

"Probably not yet, but you will. Good night, princess in the tower. I'll see you about ten on Saturday?"

"That'll be just right."

He reminded her, "I'm taking the food."

"Okay."

"You just get yourself ready—to eat, of course."

She smiled a little as she watched him with serious eyes. "Your home run won the game."

"It was for you."

"The time was thrilling. You did it all perfectly, again. Good night."

"If I kiss you—"

She pulled her head back a whole inch and said earnestly, "Don't. If you did, Hennie would spend the entire night vocally evaluating the kiss and our relationship. Just shake hands."

"I want to kiss you."

"Saturday. I will have a kiss for you on Saturday."

"Put your mind to it."

"I shall."

He smiled for the first time inside the forever vacuum in which he'd been clogged. It was a fragile, tentative, beginning smile.

She said, "I've never stopped loving you."

"You can tell me *that* and then turn around and go into Hennie's apartment and leave me out here all by myself?"

Very seriously, she told him, "Having Hennie and Jim here is the only way I could tell you such a thing and not have you attack me. You tend to be triggered."

"I promise I'll be a gentleman until you give me permission not to withhold myself from you."

"Glory be."

"Don't be snotty. I've had one hell of a time without you around, listening, advising, defying and correcting me."

"I sound like a harpie."

"Well, not *all* the time." He grinned at her.

She lifted her nose quite sassily, so of course, he

kissed her. He held her body close to his. He did a double-whammy serious, just-about-fatal kiss. It ruined them both.

His shaking hands let her go and then they had to stabilize her. She gasped, and her eyes were closed. She was uncoordinated and loose. He had to mold her back into a steady human being, female, and see to it that she surfaced again.

She said, "You dirty rat. You did it again."

And he replied, "I only meant to kiss you goodnight, you're the vampire that turned it into chaos."

She struggled to get out the words, "I—did—not."

He told her with some intensity, "That was only a See You Tomorrow kiss. You still have to kiss me good-night."

While he was hyper, her words were slow. She said, "Not this time." She was intensely serious. She turned and sought the path to the door.

It was a sidewalk for which she searched. Tyler found it for her and directed her. He took her arm into his hand, then he found he needed to put the hand on her other side. It was dark and therefore he couldn't see exactly what he was doing, and the hand slid over her breast.

"Cut it out."

He mumbled, "I won't 'cut it out,' I like it the way it is."

They came up to the laughing, chatting Hennie, and Jim, who turned and observed the approach of the divorced couple.

Jim asked, "Good heavens, man, what did you do to her?"

Tyler gave Jim a dismissive glance, but Kayla formed the words carefully. She said with some con-

centration and finally managed the words, "He…
kissed…me."

Hennie said, "Wow!"

Caught up by it all and very serious, Jim urged,
"How did he do it? Was he aggressive or kind or
what, and did he hold you formally or did—"

Tyler said, "Hush." Just the word was said, but
Tyler's look at Jim was so deadly that Jim did hush.

However, Jim's attention was riveted, his eyes were
opened wide and busily watched. His body was
tensed.

So was Tyler's Wimp.

It was the first time that Jim had ever actually wit-
nessed such a phenomenon. It was one of those rare
times when there was the opportunity for Jim to understand how a man could handle a woman.

Jim needed the information. What had Tyler done
to wreck Kayla in that way? She was so malleable
and her responses were so unreliable that a man could
have free reign!

In some agitation, Jim started urgently, "Tyler, you
have—"

And Tyler speared Jim with one deadly look and
again said, "Hush."

Jim realized how triggered Tyler was and therefore
how dangerous he was. If he stepped one step too far,
Tyler would do something really rough. Was the
knowing of handling a woman worth the risk? Probably.

But without Jim even saying one word, Tyler's
deadly look came back to him and he just watched
Jim for one endless second before his attention returned to the ruined Kayla.

She was learning to swallow with some intense

concentration. Think of that! She was so mesmerized by Tyler she'd forgotten how to swallow!

Jim almost pleaded, "Tyler—"

But Tyler came over to Jim and took hold of his shirtfront in a controlled bunch. His hand was a fist and he jolted Jim just the very least bit possible but it was a soft, deadly threat. Tyler said for the third time, "You...hush."

Probably the thing that really convinced Jim was the fact that Tyler's teeth were clenched, and his eyes were squinted almost closed. Tyler was serious. Jim was to be quiet.

So Jim subsided and paid closer attention to Tyler and to Kayla. By then, Hennie could have been abducted by aliens and Jim would never have noticed.

Kayla was pawing at Tyler! She was! No woman had ever pawed at Jim. What had caused Kayla to do that?

And Tyler was antsy and kind and soothing. He said to Kayla, "Go take a cold shower. You'll be okay."

Think of that. That slender man was driving his ex-wife crazy, and he told her to take a cold shower! What had he done to get her into such a tizzy? The woman was body hungry, and Tyler was telling her to take a cold shower!

Tyler said to Jim, "Why don't you go on home?"

With indignation, Jim straightened to object, but he looked at a very unstable man. Tyler didn't move, and his face wasn't nasty, but his eyes were slits and his teeth did not part. He was serious.

Jim said, "I have to see Henrietta to the door."

Tyler replied, "She's already inside. Go home."

"Oh. Yeah. Okay." He turned and took another, serious look at the malleable Kayla. He said, "G—"

And Tyler said, "No. Go home!"

It was not a suggestion. Tyler was serious. Tyler was two inches shorter and probably fifty pounds lighter. Those facts made Jim pause, but Tyler moved toward him in a very unkind manner.

Jim faced the fact that he was almost thirty, Tyler was younger than he and he knew how to make a woman a zombie. What had Tyler done?

Tyler moved one foot slightly. It was not a hesitation. It was a threat. He wanted Jim to shut up and leave.

Jim said, "Good night."

Neither Tyler nor Kayla replied.

Watching Jim, Tyler chose to be silent. Kayla wasn't in touch.

At the corner, Jim turned to look back. Tyler was watching him. He said in a undertoned way, "Keep going."

Just being male, Jim felt the need to hesitate. The challenge was urgent to go back and just hang around. But Tyler was serious and in a very dangerous mood. Jim lifted his hand in a friendly goodbye.

He got no response from Tyler, at all. Tyler only watched. And Jim turned to walk on off. He wondered if he would ever know all that Tyler knew about women. How had Tyler learned? How could he even find that out?

Jim gave up. He walked on back to his own apartment. He was somewhat depressed.

Alone at last...well, there were the two of them left by the front door of Hennie's apartment. Tyler considered Kayla. She was a zombie. She stood there, looking at him…waiting. He could take the zombie and she'd let him. He wanted the woman. He told her, "Go inside and get to bed. I'll see you at the picnic on Saturday."

She nodded.

He said, "Kayla. I love you."

She nodded again.

He waited while she managed the steps and opened the door. She turned and looked at him quite seriously. His own regard for her was equally serious.

Kayla went inside slowly, and she gently shut the door.

Tyler was alone. Outside in the dark, he was alone.

He went to his car and got into the driver's seat. He sat and considered Hennie's apartment door, which stayed closed.

After a time, Tyler started his car and drove slowly to his apartment—the one which once was their shared apartment. It was pristinely clean and orderly. It did not hold Kayla.

He took off his clothes and pitched them at the wicker basket. They missed, and in his new, tidy personality, he went over and picked them up. He took off the lid and put the sweaty baseball clothing into the basket. Then he went in to the shower.

Tyler stood under the warm stream and thought of the day, the game, but he mostly thought of Kayla. He looked down and the Wimp had the same idea.

He showered for some time. And he finally turned off the water and stood, drying his hair, and his body, and he brushed his teeth. He hadn't realized how tired he was. The game…and Kayla had zonked him. And that damned Jim. What the *hell* had Jim thought he was doing? All those stupid questions like *he* knew something Jim didn't!

Tyler looked at his face in the mirror and saw just how tired and ragged he was. He drank a glass of water, turned out the lights and went into the dark bedroom.

Hadn't he left the light on? He remembered the light being on. The bulb had burned out. He went into the kitchen and got a new bulb. He took it back to the bedroom and, as he turned out the hall light, he saw a lump in his bed that wasn't bunched covers.

He turned on the light with some indignation which quickly vanished. It was Kayla—there—*in his bed!*

She was there. She was there!

His lips parted and he looked very young and vulnerable. He put his hand to his chin. He had not shaved.

How like a man to think of basics.

He said, "I'll shave."

From the bed, Kayla replied, "I like whiskers."

He went carefully over to the bed and gently, carefully sat down beside her hip. He asked, "Who's that sleeping in my bed?"

"Godzilla?"

"Naw. I call him the Wimp."

She laughed as she reached out from under the covers and lay her hand on him. She heard him gasp. "Did I hurt you? I barely touched you."

"That was a thrilled gasp...not a shocked or hurt one."

"Godzilla seems very similar to being the threatening giant he was. How can you call him Wimp?"

"He's been lax and unattentive for some time. I

haven't seen him in this condition since you left. Why you?''

And she sassed as she fondled him, ''We're old friends.''

''You shouldn't neglect friends. They go into a decline.''

''He seems just like he always has.''

Tyler ignored that and went to the basics. ''How come you're here in my bed? How did you get over my double-whammy kiss so fast?''

''Well, actually, I didn't plan to come here. I was taking off my clothes to go to bed, when I found I was putting on a long coat over my naked body. And I went out the door, past Hennie who was saying something or the other, and I got into my car and—'' She shrugged remarkably so that the blanket slid a little and distracted him. She went on logically, ''—and the car just drove me over here.''

''I'll get it a full lube job tomorrow.''

She smiled slowly. ''That's what I came for. A lube job. I've been so dry and—''

''You've come to the right place. Are you sure you can handle the whiskers?''

''Let me feel.''

''Exactly what are you going to feel?''

''Well, I'll have to find your whiskers so that I can decide—''

But he'd kissed her. He groaned in agony or something terrible by just the sound, but he'd always done that when he wanted her. She was not at all alarmed—not anymore. She remembered the first—

But he'd slid down next to her, lifting her over and on top of him. He moved his hands on her bare and bumpy body. He made sounds that were hoarse and serious. He was in such agony. He was so intense.

So she was distracted. Men tend to do that to women. A woman can have a perfectly good comment or story to tell, and he just goes along and does all sorts of remarkable things and makes a woman forget what all she was going to say. Tyler was like that. Skilled that way. She was distracted...to him.

He said, "You used to like this."

And she said, "Ummmmm."

He said, "You've been neglected. These are bigger. I'll have to rub them down."

And she said, "Ahhhh."

His breathing became harsher.

Hers became quicker. She wasn't the zombie she'd been after he'd kissed her at Hennie's place, she was concentrated more and she was very intense! She was a participator. She moved her hands around on him. And she made sounds that riveted him. Her movements had the same response.

Their kisses were hungry and wet, and they just about ate each other one way or another. It was shockingly intimate. They acted like they were devouring each other. And no one was hurt or cramped or squashed. Well, she might have been but she didn't notice.

It was such intense awareness that the whole, entire place could have been torn down around them, and they would never have noticed.

They went up that thrilling spiral and shared the ultimate moment of just about oblivion before the thrilling pulsing began like the beating of a big drum. And they came floating, swirling down, back to reality...and exhaustion.

They lay for some time. They were still coupled. He'd moved just enough to release her body from some of his weight. And they lay silent and gasping, their breathing unsteady and hard, their breaths shivering with the thrills that still throbbed in their bodies…more gently then.

She said, "Wow."

He groaned.

She smoothed his damp hair and caressed his wet forehead. She said, "That'll be a hundred dollars."

"I'll find my wallet in a few minutes. You've just about finished me."

She said, "I thought we might do it again."

He snored gently.

She laughed. "You're a fraud."

He said, "Ummmm." And he moved his face to the side of her head and nuzzled her there.

Then he started nuzzling other places. He was serious.

She said, "Forget it."

And he assured her, "You don't have to do a thing. Just stay where you are. I'll handle everything."

"I just bet you would. Uh-uh, cut that out."

He gave that classic complaint, "You sure lose interest fast."

"That comment has a familiar ring."

He inquired, "Know who said it? You."

She laughed. "I can see that. What else have I said?"

"You say 'No!' a whole lot."

"When?"

"Actually, I can't recall one time."

"So. Who was the no-er?"

"Men always say women say that, and I thought if I told you so, you'd say, 'Okay. Go ahead.'"

"Why would I say that?"

"Because you love me—"

"I do? When did that happen? I don't remember falling in love with you. It seems—"

"—and you don't want me hungry and hurting."

"How can you *possibly* be 'hungry and hurting' after that voracious session of intercourse?"

He gasped, "Can you say that word out loud?"

"There's all kinds. Intercourse means many things. It means communications, sharing—"

"That's the one I like. But I want you to promise me that you'll stay away from Tom Keeper."

"He's harmless."

"I can't believe you could be that...unknowing."

"What was the word you skipped? The one you substituted as unknowing. What was the original word?"

But Tyler asked, "What were you doing with *him?*"

And she lifted her eyebrows just a tad and inquired, "With whom?"

"Tom Keeper!"

"I asked him how I could get you back."

"Oh." Then he asked carefully, "And how did he reply to that?"

"He told me to be kind to you. That you're a good man."

"Oh." Then Tyler asked, "What did he really say?"

"He told me to quit fooling around and pay attention."

"Really?"

"Really."

"Kayla, did you ever make love with him?"

"No."

"How'd you not? He's really something."

"He's okay, but he wasn't an ex-husband. I only sleep with ex-husbands."

"You haven't been...sleeping."

"Not yet."

"Can I fool around a little with you?"

"Oh, I suppose."

"What's your hand doing there?"

She leaned up and looked. "Why, how shocking!"

He laughed. "See? You're just as randy as any man. You greedy woman."

"I was shocked that you're...unclothed...and there's Godzilla all eager and attentive and waggling around—"

"I suppose you ought to calm him down."

"Why would I do that?"

He explained logically, "Because you love me."

"Why...you're right! I do love you. I hadn't realized—"

But he'd kissed her witless and she forgot what all she was going to protest and pretend and lie about.

They remarried after a while when they remembered they weren't. And the renewal marriage was a blast. Actually a whole box of champagne blew up. But it was a great party. Everyone was there. Even Tom Keeper, but that's another story.

And the two newly reweds lived happily ever after.

* * * * *

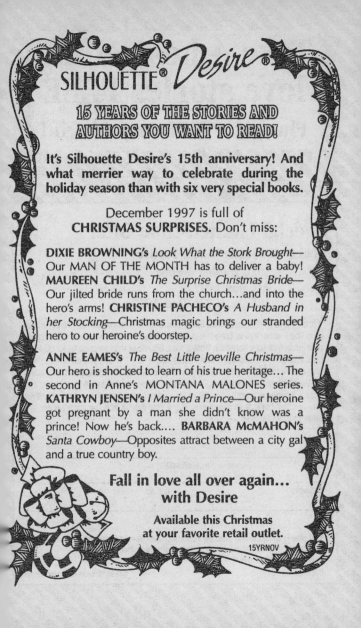

Take 4 bestselling love stories FREE

Plus get a FREE surprise gift!

SILHOUETTE WOMEN KNOW ROMANCE WHEN THEY SEE IT.

And they'll see it on **ROMANCE CLASSICS**, the new 24-hour TV channel devoted to romantic movies and original programs like the special **Romantically Speaking—Harlequin™ Goes Prime Time.**

Romantically Speaking—Harlequin™ Goes Prime Time introduces you to many of your favorite romance authors in a program developed exclusively for Harlequin® and Silhouette® readers.

Watch for **Romantically Speaking—Harlequin™ Goes Prime Time** beginning in the summer of 1997.

If you're not receiving ROMANCE CLASSICS, call your local cable operator or satellite provider and ask for it today!

ROMANCE CLASSICS

Escape to the network of your dreams.

See Ingrid Bergman and Gregory Peck in *Spellbound* on Romance Classics.

**Help us celebrate
15 years of unforgettable
romance with**

SILHOUETTE®

Desire®

You could win a genuine lead crystal vase, or one of 4 sets of 4 crystal champagne flutes! Every prize is made of hand-blown, hand-cut crystal, with each process handled by master craftsmen. We're making these fantastic gifts available to be won by you, just for helping us celebrate 15 years of the best romance reading around!

DESIRE CRYSTAL SWEEPSTAKES
OFFICIAL ENTRY FORM

To enter, complete an Official Entry Form or 3" x 5" card by hand printing the words "Desire Crystal Sweepstakes," your name and address thereon and mailing it to: in the U.S., Desire Crystal Sweepstakes, P.O. Box 9076, Buffalo, NY 14269-9076; in Canada, Desire Crystal Sweepstakes, P.O. Box 637, Fort Erie, Ontario L2A 5X3. Limit: one entry per envelope, one prize to an individual, family or organization. Entries must be sent via first-class mail and be received no later than 12/31/97. No responsibility is assumed for lost, late, misdirected or nondelivered mail.

DESIRE CRYSTAL SWEEPSTAKES
OFFICIAL ENTRY FORM

Name: _____

Address: _____

City: _____

State/Prov.: _____   Zip/Postal Code: _____

KFO

15YRENTRY

Desire Crystal Sweepstakes
Official Rules—No Purchase Necessary

To enter, complete an Official Entry Form or 3" x 5" card by hand printing the words "Desire Crystal Sweepstakes," your name and address thereon and mailing it to: in the U.S., Desire Crystal Sweepstakes, P.O. Box 9076, Buffalo, NY 14269-9076; in Canada, Desire Crystal Sweepstakes, P.O. Box 637, Fort Erie, Ontario L2A 5X3. Limit: one entry per envelope, one prize to an individual, family or organization. Entries must be sent via first-class mail and be received no later than 12/31/97. No responsibility is assumed for lost, late, misdirected or nondelivered mail.

Winners will be selected in random drawings (to be conducted no later than 1/31/98) from among all eligible entries received by D. L. Blair, Inc., an independent judging organization whose decisions are final. The prizes and their approximate values are: Grand Prize—a Mikasa Crystal Vase ($140 U.S.); 4 Second Prizes—a set of 4 Mikasa Crystal Champagne Flutes ($50 U.S. each set).

Sweepstakes offer is open only to residents of the U.S. (except Puerto Rico) and Canada who are 18 years of age or older, except employees and immediate family members of Harlequin Enterprises, Ltd., their affiliates, subsidiaries and all other agencies, entities and persons connected with the use, marketing or conduct of this sweepstakes. All applicable laws and regulations apply. Offer void wherever prohibited by law. Taxes and/or duties on prizes are the sole responsibility of the winners. Any litigation within the province of Quebec respecting the conduct and awarding of a prize in this sweepstakes may be submitted to the Régie des alcools, des courses et des jeux. All prizes will be awarded; winners will be notified by mail. No substitution for prizes is permitted. Odds of winning are dependent upon the number of eligible entries received.

Any prize or prize notification returned as undeliverable may result in the awarding of that prize to an alternative winner. By acceptance of their prize, winners consent to use of their names, photographs or likenesses for purposes of advertising, trade and promotion on behalf of Harlequin Enterprises, Ltd., without further compensation unless prohibited by law. In order to win a prize, residents of Canada will be required to correctly answer a time-limited, arithmetical skill-testing question administered by mail.

For a list of winners (available after January 31, 1998), send a separate stamped, self-addressed envelope to: Desire Crystal Sweepstakes 5309 Winners, P.O. Box 4200, Blair, NE 68009-4200, U.S.A.

Sweepstakes sponsored by Harlequin Enterprises Ltd., P.O. Box 9042, Buffalo, NY 14269-9042.

15YRRULE

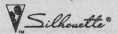